RIVERBEND FRIENDS™

Real, Not Perfect
Searching for Normal
The Me You See
Chasing the Spotlight

SEARCHING FOR NORMAL

Searching for Normal

RIVERBEND FRIENDS™

C. J. Darlington

CREATED BY

Lissa Halls Johnson

FOCUS
ON THE FAMILY®

A Focus on the Family Resource
Published by Tyndale House Publishers

Searching for Normal

Copyright © 2021 by Focus on the Family. All rights reserved.

A Focus on the Family book published by Tyndale House Publishers, Carol Stream, Illinois 60188

Focus on the Family and the accompanying logo and design are federally registered trademarks and *Riverbend Friends* is a trademark of Focus on the Family, 8605 Explorer Drive, Colorado Springs, CO 80920.

TYNDALE and Tyndale's quill logo are registered trademarks of Tyndale House Ministries

Scripture quotations are from The ESV® Bible (The Holy Bible, English Standard Version®), copyright © 2001 by Crossway, a publishing ministry of Good News Publishers. Used by permission. All rights reserved.

Cover design by Mike Harrigan

The characters and events in this story are fictional. Any resemblance to actual persons or events is coincidental.

For manufacturing information regarding this product, please call 1-800-323-9400.

For information about special discounts for bulk purchases, please contact Tyndale House Publishers at csresponse@tyndale.com, or call 1-855-277-9400.

ISBN 978-1-58997-705-1

Library of Congress Cataloging-in-Publication Data can be found at www.loc.gov.

Printed in the United States of America

27	26	25	24	23	22	21
7	6	5	4	3	2	1

Chapter

1

I wished my grandmother would yell at me. Or say *something*. Even a scolding about how I needed to stop slouching or speak up or quit being so sensitive would've been better than the icy silence that filled the SUV. So I stayed quiet too, watching the green street signs pass by us in the darkness and listening to the squeaky windshield wipers keep rhythmic time. Grams didn't have to say a word to convey her disappointment. The silence screamed what she couldn't say: *Shay Mitchell, you're a loser.*

I glanced over at the older woman, her graying hair coiffed and styled like she was heading to a gala at the country club rather than pawning off her granddaughter. I'd been staying off and on with my Aunt Laura since school started, but now it was going to be official. My grandparents had made that very clear. Screw up like I had, and you end up alone. Or at least out of their house.

When we were nearly at the bookstore my aunt owned, I almost spoke up. Wouldn't speaking my mind be better than holding everything inside? That's what my friend Amelia would definitely

1

say. And Izzy and Tessa would probably agree too, though Tessa might at least understand why I was regularly labeled shy. But people who called me that usually didn't understand I was often quiet just because it sometimes took me a while to figure out what I wanted to say. By the time I did, everyone else had usually moved on. I wasn't antisocial. I just needed to socialize with the right people. People who got me. Unfortunately, most didn't.

"Did you pack your Bible?"

I closed my eyes for a second before waving toward the back seat currently loaded with my meager belongings. "I packed *everything*."

"Well, you seem to have forgotten *everything* your dad taught you."

In my heart I tried to remember that even though I'd lost my dad six months ago, she'd lost her only son. Her callousness made sense, but it didn't hurt any less.

"Your aunt's sacrificing a lot to take you in."

Like Grams hadn't told me that about a million times in the last week.

I shrugged.

My grandmother shook her head.

About the sum of our relationship these days. I could barely remember the fun Christmases where we'd trek to the tree farm and cut down our own tree and my grandfather made his famous eggnog even my dad couldn't replicate. Or every year on my birthday when we'd all go camping with the horses.

I rubbed the small scar hidden under my hairline. I wanted to say I was sorry for the trouble I'd caused them, and how I wished things were different. I would do anything to go back and change what happened. But instead, I did what I always did—I kept it all inside.

Grams turned into the back parking lot of Booked Up, and a burst of adrenaline flickered across my chest. I actually liked my aunt, mostly because she left me alone a lot of the time. This nervousness was rooted at a deeper level. I'd never really thrived on uncertainty or the unknown. That was for people like my dad, the brilliant artist and book-cover designer by day and adrenaline junkie by night. Dad had *skydive over every continent* plastered at the top of his bucket list. *Had* being the operative word.

I climbed out of the SUV and opened the back door, grabbing my overfilled suitcase and duffel bag. It was still raining, but I didn't really care.

Grams carefully unfurled her umbrella before stepping out. "Shay, your hair!"

I shrugged again. My hair was the least of my concerns pretty much every day. A little water wouldn't hurt it.

I made two wet trips from the SUV to the bookstore storeroom before Grams found Aunt Laura somewhere in the store. She knew we were coming, but I didn't expect her to be waiting. Despite the fact that she was a successful entrepreneur in her thirties, my aunt was late to nearly everything. It would almost be an endearing quality if it didn't mean that I ended up late everywhere too.

Aunt Laura rushed into the storeroom behind my grandmother, tucking strands of her shoulder-length, wavy dark hair behind her ears. She'd dyed a thin strip of it red, and today she rocked the professional, entrepreneurial-woman look in skinny jeans and a blazer. I glanced down at my own worn jeans and cowboy boots. One small positive. Maybe some of her style would rub off on me.

"Sorry," Aunt Laura said. "Lost track of the time."

I managed a smile. My grandmother did not.

Aunt Laura took my duffel from me and gave me a quick pat on the shoulder. No hug, which also didn't surprise me. Physical affection was a scarce commodity with my aunt, though not because she didn't care. Hugs just weren't her thing.

"I'll catch up with you," Aunt Laura said to me.

Which meant she and my grandmother wanted to talk about me.

I started to walk away still lugging my suitcase, but then I hesitated as a twinge of sadness touched me. My grandmother and I might not be on the best of terms, but she was still my grandmother.

"See ya, Grams," I said.

But my grandmother had already turned her back.

The bookstore smelled like paper and French roast coffee, and even though my suitcase had wheels, I chose to carry it. At seven o'clock the place was crowded, and I hated the attention the noisy wheels would bring. I could've used the outside entrance to get to my aunt's apartment above the bookstore, but I didn't relish carrying luggage up a flight of slippery wooden stairs. So through the bookstore I went, hoping to avoid eye contact with customers.

I weaved my way around a woman perusing the shelves of used books, a dripping umbrella hanging from her hand. Aunt Laura would lose it if she saw that. It was going to stain the—

"Shay!"

I almost pretended I didn't hear the girl calling my name.

"Hey, Shay!" another girl called.

I reluctantly turned toward the voices. It wasn't that I didn't care about my friends. I just didn't want them to see me like this. I felt too raw, and I was carrying a suitcase. All of them already thought I lived with my aunt since I'd stayed with her a few times when my grandparents vacationed at their cabin. I'd never corrected their assumptions.

I quickly tucked my suitcase beside an endcap displaying Jane Austen classics and walked over to the alcove with the love seat and beanbag chairs my friends always snagged when they were here.

That's when I remembered all the Snapchat notifications I'd gotten earlier and had neglected to check. They'd probably been trying to wrangle me into one of their outside-of-class drama team meetings.

"Didn't you get my message?" Amelia waved her phone in my direction, pulling her purple-yoga-pant-clad leg underneath herself on the love seat.

Note to self: Remind her not to leave her phone in the bookstore. Amelia notoriously forgot the thing everywhere, and I didn't want to have to remember to bring it to school tomorrow.

"Um . . . no." I pulled my phone from my back pocket. Yep. At least ten notifications.

I hadn't been very involved with social media before I met these girls, and while it was kinda fun to actually have friends to interact with, there were times I wanted to turn my phone completely off and curl up with a good book. Sometimes I did.

"What if we'd really needed to reach you?" Amelia's eyebrows cocked. She reminded me of her family's Labradoodle—bouncy, boisterous, and ready to have a good time. I envied her zest for life.

"This is Shay we're talking about," Izzy chimed in, leaning backward in her beanbag chair to stare up at me. I spotted a copy of *Martha Stewart's Cookie Perfection* in her lap and hoped I might soon be on the receiving end of one of her baking experiments. Even Izzy's cooking rejects were culinary delights to me.

"Admit it. You hate your phone," Amelia said.

Normally I didn't mind their teasing. It made me feel like they cared about me. And I *did* dislike technology, but today I didn't feel like pretending I was happy. I glanced at Tessa, who shared the love seat with Amelia, holding a coffee cup with both hands. She was the only one of us who drank coffee and liked it. It unnerved me how she could usually tell when I was uncomfortable, but today I hoped she did and could steer the others onto topics that didn't involve me.

"I'm no Luddite," I said and immediately wished I hadn't.

Sometimes I used big words from my reading habits, often pronounced incorrectly. I didn't even think about it, but I hoped they didn't assume I was trying to sound smarter than them, because that was totally not the case. All of my friends got better grades than I did.

Amelia cocked her head. "Lu . . . what?"

Izzy pecked at her phone with her index finger. "Bingo! Dictionary app, girls. I need it with these two." She pointed at Tessa and me. "Luddite means . . . hold on . . . 'a person opposed to new technology or ways of working.'"

All three of them laughed.

"You were saying, Shay?"

"Okay, okay." I couldn't help but join in.

"So." Amelia scooted to the edge of the love seat, clapping her hands together. "We're talking about a Christmas play."

Tessa took a sip from her mug. "We?"

"I'm telling you, it will be fun!"

"But we just finished the One Act," I said.

"Exactly!" Amelia waved her hand in the air. "We're on a roll."

"I don't—"

"Shay, come on. You gotta help me out here."

Izzy picked up her cookbook, flipping through the pages. "I'm staying out of this."

I took a deep breath and crossed my arms. I'd only taken Intro to Drama because I was required to take a fine arts class, and it was the only one that fit my schedule. I didn't hate creativity or the arts per se, but I honestly hated performing in front of anyone. Even my friends. They had to know that by now. I was the weakest link in our drama group, and I was surprised they hadn't asked me to leave.

"You were great playing Lena," Amelia said.

I scoffed. "Liar."

"No, seriously. I could feel your anger. It was . . ."

"Terrible?"

Amelia gestured for me to sit in the empty beanbag chair by her, but the last thing I wanted to do was discuss my performance. My friends had no idea why I'd struggled so much with Lena. At first I hadn't even been sure myself. If anything, I actually related to the fictional girl's feelings. Maybe that was why. Every time I'd tried to channel Lena's anger, I felt the rage inside myself, and it had scared me. I felt if I truly got into her character, I might take it too far.

"I'm sorry I missed your messages," I said, glancing at my feet. The leather of my boots was soaked, and I could feel the moisture seeping through my socks. I wanted to tell her the truth, that I was too tired and emotionally spent to handle any intelligent conversation, even with my friends. But instead, what did I do?

With a groan, I slumped down in the beanbag chair.

Tessa nudged my shoulder. "You okay?"

I nodded. I wasn't lying entirely. Not really. Somehow I'd make it through this. I just wasn't sure how much of me would be left in the end. My dad, he was the one who . . . no. I couldn't afford to think about Dad right now.

"Guys, a Christmas play. We can do it." Amelia's eyes sparked. She really was into this drama thing.

"Has anyone talked to Ms. Larkin?" Izzy asked, still flipping through the cookbook.

Our drama teacher reminded me of a beautiful Afghan Hound, her hair and dresses all flowy and elegant. Izzy and Amelia had wondered aloud about why the woman was still single, but I thought it was cool she didn't need a guy in her life to complete her.

"Are we really thinking about Christmas already?" I leaned back and closed my eyes. I was not one to fall asleep anywhere, but the warm bookstore air and comfortable beanbag chair were enticing.

"Yes, Shay, we are." Amelia poked me in the ribs with her foot. "How else will we have time to memorize our lines and—"

Tessa groaned. "I'm with Shay. I barely have time for the swim team. I can't add anything else to my plate right now."

"And Alex," Izzy teased. "A girl's gotta make time for the important things in life."

I opened my eyes and distinctly saw a pink hue spread across Tessa's cheeks at the mention of her boyfriend. Even I, who was staunchly the Jo March of our group, thought Alex and Tessa made a cute couple. He had helped Tessa through a lot in the last few weeks, proving he was not only a great boyfriend, but also a true-blue friend to her.

Tessa took a sip of her coffee, probably to give herself a second to think. "You guys are just as important," she finally said.

"Mm-hmm," Izzy mumbled, but there was a smile pulling at her mouth.

"So what's with the suitcase?"

I tensed at Amelia's question. "What suitcase?"

"The one you were carrying," Amelia said.

"I . . ."

"Going on a weekend trip?"

I really wanted to lie. I did. But if my dad taught me anything, it was that the truth never hurt anyone. Which wasn't exactly true, if you asked me, but since I knew how God felt about lying, I decided I would either have to find a way not to answer or tell them the real story. Because right now I think they just assumed my parents weren't in the picture because there was some nasty custody battle or something.

I looked around at our little group. I'd never been good at making friends, but here I finally had a few and I was thinking about lying to them? What kind of friendship was that? I just didn't want their pity. I'd already felt it before when, one time, Izzy gushed about how fun her family could be, and then quickly changed the subject. Or even when Tessa opened up about her parents' divorce, I could feel that she hesitated. At least she *had* a father, even if he was a jerk sometimes. What they didn't realize was that I didn't want them to treat me any differently. I wanted them to be happy and enjoy their lives. My dad wasn't coming back, and there was nothing anyone could do about it. End of story.

But at some point, I really was going to have to tell them.

"I'm moving in with my aunt," I said softly.

My friends all stopped for a beat. Izzy closed her book. Amelia scooted even farther to the edge of the love seat, and Tessa set down her coffee mug.

"Don't you already live with her?" Izzy asked.

"I have been staying with her sometimes," I said, wishing I wasn't sitting in the beanbag chair anymore where my friends could stare at me easier. "Officially I've been living with my grand-parents, but now I'm moving in with Aunt Laura."

"But . . . why?"

Leave it to Amelia to ask the obvious question probably shooting through all of their minds. The one I wasn't prepared to answer and probably never would be.

I climbed to my feet. "Just because."

Amelia started to ask me again, but Tessa elbowed her.

Izzy's eyes brightened. "Need any help unpacking?"

I'd only known these girls for two and a half months, and I hadn't gotten to the invite-them-over-to-my-house stage. *Unpacking my clothes? Um, no thanks.* I appreciated the offer, I really did, but I needed time to myself.

"I'm good," I said. "And I really have to get going."

Without thinking, I turned on my heels, pulled my suitcase from behind the display and headed to the stairs leading to my aunt's apartment.

I wondered if my friends realized only one of those statements was true.

Chapter

2

I PUSHED OPEN THE DOOR to my aunt's apartment and nearly jumped out of my skin. A huge, lanky dog leapt up from the floor and ran over to greet me, tail swinging and hitting everything it passed. The sofa, the end table, a stack of books—I scooted inside and shut the door.

"Hey, there. Who are you?"

The brindle-colored dog, whose head nearly reached my waist, sniffed me, then went to my suitcase. I knew right away he was a greyhound, but I did not know why he was in my aunt's apartment.

After a thorough inspection of my gear with his nose, the dog bounded off and grabbed a squeaky toy in the shape of a teddy bear. I knelt in front of him and grabbed for the toy, which seemed to please him to no end. He darted out of my reach and then stopped with the bear hanging from his mouth, as if waiting for me to try again. I did.

When my aunt walked in a few minutes later, we were both still on the floor.

"So you met him?" Aunt Laura dumped my duffel bag next to my suitcase and came over to us.

"He's adorable."

My aunt chuckled. "Sixty-eight pounds of sweetness. His name's Stanley."

"Why didn't you tell me you got a dog?"

Stanley ran over to my aunt.

"Wanted to surprise you."

I stood up. I'd forgotten all about being tired while I played with the dog, but the blanket of exhaustion draped over me once again.

Aunt Laura held up a hand. "Before you get too excited, he's a foster. Not actually mine."

Stanley bounded to me again, leaning against my leg and throwing me off balance. His chocolate eyes stared into mine. After Panda, my black Lab, died, I'd begged first my dad and then my grandparents for a dog. I thought I'd finally talked them into it, but then I got in trouble and any talk of pets tanked with my hope. My aunt knew all this.

"How long do you have him?"

"Could be a few days or a few weeks." Aunt Laura smiled. "So basically, don't get too attached."

Like that was going to be easy. I was already smitten. "But don't greyhounds chase cats?"

My aunt's tortoiseshell cat, Matilda, often roamed the bookstore, but she always returned to the apartment at the end of the day. When I was here, she usually slept on my bed.

"Not all of them," Aunt Laura said. "He was cat-tested and gives Matilda her space. All it took was one swipe at his nose to remind him of his place."

I dropped onto the sofa and sighed. Speaking of space, the

apartment was barely large enough for my aunt. Me showing up had to cramp her lifestyle. The second bedroom had been her office and library, and she'd had to put stuff in storage so I could have a place to sleep.

"I'm sorry about all this," I said.

"About what?"

"Me."

My aunt crossed her arms. "Shay."

"This isn't what you signed up for."

Sitting down beside me, Aunt Laura took a moment before she spoke. Stanley immediately jumped up and positioned himself between us, his warm head resting on my lap. I stroked his velvety ears. It was probably better to get this conversation over with.

"Listen, kid." Aunt Laura pet Stanley too. "*You* didn't sign up for this either. But that doesn't mean we can't make it work."

Grams's words about my aunt sacrificing to keep me here rang in my ears. The last thing I wanted was to be a burden, but that was clearly what I was. Aunt Laura was an independent business-woman who'd purposely kept her life simple and no-nonsense to pursue her passion. Throwing a teenager in the mix was a recipe for disappointment. Just ask my grandmother.

Aunt Laura gave my leg a quick pat. "It'll work."

I nodded, but I didn't really believe it. Lately it felt like every-thing I touched ended up tainted. I couldn't even figure out how to *act* properly in drama class. Maybe I'd never fit in.

"Let's give it our best shot, okay?"

I'd given my best at my grandparents'. Look where that got me.

"Your friends were asking about you earlier." Aunt Laura got up and walked over to the kitchen area of the open-floor-plan room that was also the living room and dining room, and now my aunt's office, too.

"I caught up with them."

"They seem like nice girls."

"Yep." I pulled out my phone and was about to scroll through my YouTube feed, but then caught my aunt's disapproving glance. I imagined it was what my mother, Aunt Laura's older sister, would've done, though there was no way for me to know for sure. She'd died when I was a baby.

"You met them in drama class, right?"

I tried to remember if I'd spoken to any of the girls before then or not. I'd seen them around, but I think that was it. I'd been so self-conscious for most of the class I could barely remember their names afterward, but Amelia pulled me over to their lunch table the next day, and I hadn't eaten lunch in peace since. I smiled at the thought. I didn't mind having friends. Not at all. But sometimes I just wanted to be alone.

"They didn't know I wasn't living with you," I say softly.

My aunt opened the fridge and pulled out a take-out container. "What had you told them?"

"Nothing," I said. "They just assumed."

"Well, I've known them longer than you." Aunt Laura pointed at the container and then at me. I shook my head. "Millie's my magazine girl, though I think she bought a novel last time she was here."

"Amelia."

"Hmm?"

"She prefers Amelia, not Millie."

Aunt Laura popped the container in the microwave. "Izzy's definitely my best cookbook customer, and Tessa . . . she doesn't usually buy anything. Just browses or does her schoolwork, but that's okay."

Sounded like my friends. We didn't exactly live in a small town, but I guess owning a bookstore gave you insight on at least the people who frequented your establishment, and my aunt had been here six years.

I surreptitiously pulled up YouTube again on my phone. My

recommendations were mostly animal related, and the first one grabbed my interest. "Mason King coming to a town near you!" It was a video marketing the tour schedule for one of my favorite horse trainers. I clicked on the preview. My aunt gave me another look, but this time she just turned on the microwave.

Aunt Laura came over to the sofa again as the video played. She set her silverware and a glass of water on the end table. She wasn't really much of a cook. She could make some basic dishes . . . pasta, stir fry, salad. Mostly she just ate out or ordered in, but I knew she wanted to make changes in that department now that I was here.

I turned the phone toward her, hoping that by sharing it would make it okay to be watching a video when I probably should be having a conversation. The promo continued to play, showing Mason working a horse in a round pen. Then there was a shot of him riding a horse deemed too dangerous to handle, in an arena crammed with fans.

"He's like America's Clinton Anderson," I said, referencing a popular Australian horse trainer.

Something changed on my aunt's face as she watched a few seconds of the video. Her eyes narrowed. "This is the trainer you were telling me about?"

"I wish he was coming somewhere close to us," I said softly and then got out of YouTube after the video finished. I didn't want to ruffle my aunt any more than I apparently had, though I couldn't figure out what I'd done.

"I'm glad he's not."

"What? Why?"

The microwave dinged, and Aunt Laura went over and pulled out her steaming meal of leftovers. The smell of pad Thai wafted toward me and made me regret not accepting the offer to share. I'd have to find something else for dinner.

Aunt Laura didn't answer me, and I wasn't sure if I should press her.

"I've never liked those types of trainers," she said. "Selling halters with their logos for fifty bucks when you can get them for ten without. Seems dishonest."

"Not if they're good quality."

"Making promises they can't keep." Aunt Laura sat down on the couch, and Stanley immediately turned around and faced her, his nose sniffing the air. Maybe he liked Thai food as well.

"Luring in unsuspecting women who are more than happy to shell out their cash and buy his overpriced, overhyped training system, saddles, and who knows what else!"

I turned toward my aunt, not sure where her outrage was coming from. She'd never acted particularly interested in horses, and I didn't realize she knew enough about them to even have this argument. I tried not to act like I felt miffed that she was criticizing a horseman I'd admired for years. I know the horse industry certainly had its share of con men—didn't any industry? But Mason King was different. It was clear he actually cared about the horses, and the results he accomplished were real.

"Sorry," Aunt Laura said.

"He's not like that."

"And how do you know?"

"I . . ." *It wasn't like I knew the man personally, but still; I knew.*

"Just remember not to believe everything on the Internet."

I almost rolled my eyes. She was talking to me like I was five, not fifteen. But I didn't want to spoil the evening or give my aunt any reason to regret my presence.

"I'll be in my room," I said, deciding to unpack my things and cool down.

A few minutes later, bedroom door closed, I still hadn't unpacked. I dropped onto the bed and lay on my back trying to decide what was bothering me.

Chapter
3

AMELIA HAD LEFT HER PHONE in the bookstore. The next morning as I was about to head out the door, Aunt Laura dangled it in front of me, and with an eye roll I stuffed it into my backpack. I hadn't slept well but didn't tell my aunt.

I walked to school most days; my choice now that I lived close enough. It was my thinking time, and I could be completely alone with my thoughts. I steered around a parka-bundled man clutching a thermal coffee mug. He looked like an Alaskan malamute or a Siberian husky that belonged in the arctic tundra.

My phone chirped as a text came in. Then it chirped again. I'd think it was Amelia if I didn't already have her phone. She'd sent me eight out of the ten Snapchat messages last night. I hadn't responded to any of them. *Maybe I was a Luddite after all.*

The text read: Forgot phone!!! Help!!! Texting from my mom's!

I quickly tapped a reply: Got it. Will bring.

THANK YOU SO MUCH!!! She included five different emojis. A wild smiley face, hands clapping, a birthday cake (no idea why), a thumbs-up, and her favorite for whenever she texted me: a dog. Her emoji love drove Tessa nuts, but in a silly way they actually made me happier.

The walk to school was cold, and I stuffed my hands in my coat pockets, where I'd stashed two hand warmers courtesy of my aunt. I still felt like a waddling penguin when I arrived at school. Maybe I could get over myself and ask Tessa to pick me up on the really cold mornings now that she had her license.

Someone bumped me in the shoulder.

Two junior girls, Kelsey and Jade, stepped into my field of vision, and my stomach clenched. I wasn't sure why they seemed to have it in for me. Last week I was almost sure one of them tried to trip me in the cafeteria, but I couldn't prove it.

"Hey," Kelsey said, flipping her Irish setter mane of auburn hair over her shoulder and rewrapping her cashmere scarf around her neck. "Almost didn't see you."

I shifted my backpack. "Cold enough?"

I hate how I resort to small talk when I'm uncomfortable, but in the moment it's what came out.

Kelsey laughed, and her sidekick, Jade, who could've been the little sister of that actress who played Mulan, echoed. Both of them wore down parkas with fur trim that definitely weren't from L.L.Bean, though I noted a stray feather pushing through the seam near Jade's elbow. For some reason that was satisfying.

"What'd you say?" Kelsey said.

"Nothing."

Jade glanced at Kelsey. "I'm toasty warm. You?"

"Totally," Kelsey said. "But I didn't walk to school."

No, you didn't. You both got your own cars from your daddies the day you turned sixteen, and you let me know it the first day I got here.

"I like to walk," I said.

Kelsey gave me a compassionless look, one that said I was pathetic.

"It's refreshing," I said. I was trying to sound much more confident than I felt. I knew what they were doing, but I could never bring myself to stop them.

"Exercise never hurt anyone," I added.

"Certainly not you," Kelsey said.

"Watch out," Jade chimed in. "Hang out with big girls and you end up looking like them."

Wait, is she making fun of Amelia, too?

I hated that I didn't stick up for her in that moment, but I was too mortified to respond. I'd never been a skinny girl, but I wasn't overweight. At least I didn't think so. I tried to step away from the girls, but they placed themselves directly in my path on the sidewalk.

"Got long underwear on under those jeans?" Kelsey waved at my pants, a newer pair of Wranglers my grandparents bought me when I first went to live with them. I loved them because I could wear them to school and ride in them too—if I ever wanted. Not that I'd had much chance to ride, let alone even see a horse for a long time.

"That might explain the extra padding," Jade said.

"I'm not that cold," I said.

"So you *do* wear long underwear." Jade pulled out her phone and snapped a picture of me before I could object.

"Hey."

"Hey what? You're lookin' good. Don't ya want the world—or even better, the boys—to see? Oh . . . wait." Jade gave her friend a conspiratorial glance. "Maybe that's not an issue for you."

I closed my eyes for a split second as I felt a fire sparking inside of me. I was just trying to be myself. I didn't choose my clothes for attention potential.

"Nah, she doesn't have to worry about that," Kelsey said.

Jade was already poking at her phone, posting the photo who knows where before she walked into school. I glanced down at myself, rethinking my clothing choices. I wore my waterproof hiking boots and a Carhartt coat over my hoodie. It wasn't like our school was in the ritziest area of town or anything. Other girls wore jeans. But maybe I should try to fit in a little bit and at least buy a pair of . . . well . . . a pair of what? I didn't even know what was "it" these days to have a clue what would blend in. And really, that's all I wanted. To melt into the background and be left alone.

"Read any good books lately?" Kelsey stood a couple of inches above me, and it almost seemed like this morning she was standing on tiptoes to appear even taller.

"I gotta get going," I said.

"But I thought you loved books."

"We're gonna be late."

Kelsey glanced at her iPhone. "Chill. There's time."

"So seriously," Jade said. "Any recommendations?" She flipped her hair like Kelsey had earlier, and I tried not to envy how dark and beautiful it was. *Is it naturally lustrous, or does she do something to it?* I thought of my grandmother scolding me for not covering my head in the rain, and I hoped the frizz hadn't carried over into today. I'd simply brushed mine and pulled it back into a ponytail like I always did.

I shrugged. "Haven't read much lately."

"Why not?"

"Just 'cause."

Kelsey nodded toward Jade. "Maybe a self-help title. Something on how to be pretty when you're not."

"Or living with relatives who aren't your parents," Jade said. "What would you recommend along those lines? I bet your aunt has a million of those in stock."

The angry fire rose in me again. I could feel it swelling in my belly, and I didn't stop it. I knew I should, but I didn't.

"I'm sorry, did I say something wrong?" Kelsey's eyebrows lowered as she fiddled with her scarf once more.

"Too soon, right?" Jade tucked her phone away. "I can sometimes be insensitive like that. I forgot you've only been here a couple of months. I gotta know though. Why don't your parents want you?"

I swallowed. "They wanted me."

"Then why aren't you living with them?"

"My dad was a single parent." The second I said it, I regretted my words. They didn't deserve to know anything about me, much less something personal. It would only be ammunition.

"What, your mom ditched you?"

Kelsey elbowed Jade. "Be nice. That must've been tough." There was a note of what sounded like real sympathy in her tone, but I knew better. I also know better than to let them goad me, but how am I supposed to stop it? Walking away would make me look weak, and people like them prey on that. But standing up for myself was also asking for trouble and might make them push me even more.

"Not growing up with a mom to talk to must've been hard too." Jade smiled. "Did your dad teach you about periods and stuff?"

Kelsey pretended to punch Jade's arm. "Ew, awkward!"

The fire burned stronger, and now I felt an embarrassed blush hitting my cheeks. Who else was supposed to teach me? My dad had always been cool about stuff like that and made sure I was comfortable in a potentially weird situation, but still.

I squared my shoulders and stared into Kelsey's green eyes. She stared back. I saw something in them then. It was the intense look of a cat before she sprung on a mouse, and Kelsey clearly thought I was the rodent.

"Get out of my way," I said, trying not to clench my teeth. I kept my voice even and calm, but it was becoming harder to shove down the fire. *Breathe.* That's what my grandmother had advised me, probably wisdom from a yoga class or something.

But I didn't feel like breathing. I felt like punching.

Kelsey's nose wrinkled. "What? I was just asking for a book recommendation."

I started to sidle past her, but she stepped directly in front of me.

"Seriously, what's your problem?"

Before I could respond, another girl came up beside me. Amelia hooked her arm in mine and pulled me away, waving over her shoulder at Kelsey and Jade as she did.

"You have no idea how I've suffered," she said, not skipping a beat once we were alone at the curb. "Please tell me you have it."

I couldn't take in oxygen for a second as guilt smacked me in the gut at how close I'd been to losing it, not to mention letting those girls talk about Amelia like they did. *How could I have let myself go there again?*

"Earth to Shay."

"Sorry." I faced my friend.

"What's wrong?"

"Nothing." The temperature inside me dialed down a few degrees. "Do I have what?"

"My phone!"

I robotically fumbled in my backpack.

"Why's your hand shaking?"

Dang it, does Amelia have to notice everything?

I found her cell and handed it over, and she proceeded to pull me into a huge bear hug. "Thank you!"

I was weird with hugs. I had to really know someone, love them even, to enjoy a hug, but Amelia hugged me the first day we met. I was so taken aback, it probably felt to her like she was hugging a mannequin, and I'd worried I'd offended her. But when Amelia hugged you, she really *hugged* you since there was a lot of her to hug. Now I always tried to hug back.

She finally let me go, placing the back of her hand on her forehead in a dramatic gesture. "Last night I reached for my precious, and she wasn't there. Then this morning, my nightstand was bare!"

"It's too early for rhymes," I said, finally breaking a smile.

"Oh, I'm not done."

Izzy joined us before Amelia could continue waxing poetic. "*Hola, amigas!*"

I pointed at her knee-high, lace up boots and gave her a thumbs up. Izzy often wore leggings (she disliked jeans, but I decided not to hold that against her), and these boots had become one of her staples. She totally wasn't up on fashion, according to her, but I was always impressed with how she somehow managed to look fashionable. Not that I'd know if a piece of clothing was in fashion if it bit me in the—

"Shay saved me, that's what's up." Amelia donned the dramatic voice again and waved her phone, but I could see her hint of a smile.

Other way around, Amelia.

I glanced over at Kelsey and Jade. They were both watching me. Kelsey puffed out her cheeks and pointed at Amelia, and I turned away. I should've known better. Should've *been* better. *Hadn't I learned anything over what happened this summer?*

I tried to focus all my attention on my friends. Izzy looked confused, and I held my hand to my ear like it was a phone receiver.

"Again?" Izzy asked.

"Yep."

I willed myself to switch gears. Classes started soon, and Izzy and I had World History together first hour. We needed to hustle, but I didn't feel like hustling. I didn't feel like doing anything, actually. But I slapped on a smile, said goodbye to Amelia and Izzy, who had to run to the bathroom, and promised Amelia I'd see her later in drama class.

When I was by myself again, I dropped the smile.

Chapter

4

Except for first and second grade, I'd done online school, so the high school life was new to me. I hated how much time we wasted, but walking down the school hallway was the real torture. It didn't matter how many times I made the trek, I still felt like a lab rat. The students were the scientists studying me. When I confided in Amelia one time, she said she felt similarly but pretended she was Julia Roberts strutting down the red carpet at a premiere. It seemed to work for her. Me? I didn't want to be an actress. I didn't even want to be in drama class. The best I could pretend was that I didn't care.

Most days it didn't work.

My locker was on the same wall as Tessa's, and part of me hoped I'd run into her. But she was usually early to her classes. I was often late, so we didn't cross paths in the hall as often as you'd think.

Today she was waiting for me at my locker.

She smiled. "Hey."

"Hey, back."

"About last night," Tessa said. "Sorry if we ambushed you."

"It's okay." I opened my locker and stuffed my backpack inside. A lot of the students didn't even use their lockers, keeping their packs with them at all times, but I didn't like lugging such a heavy bag around from class to class.

Tessa held her English book to her chest and leaned against the locker next to mine. I couldn't remember the name of the guy who owned it. Just that he always wore way too much cologne, and I could faintly smell it wafting out the vents.

"I didn't realize you lived with your grandparents," Tessa said.

I shrugged.

"Shay, it's a big deal, I know."

No, actually, I didn't think she did know, but she was trying. I could give her that. She'd been through a lot with her parents' divorce and her dad moving out.

"Are you okay with it?"

I managed a sarcastic laugh. I wanted to say I didn't have a choice, but instead I just responded, "I'm fine."

"That's what I always used to say."

"My aunt's a good person. The bookstore's interesting, I can walk to school, and she has a dog now. It's not terrible."

Tessa nodded. "But it's a big change."

"I should've told you guys."

"Your aunt does seem nice."

"I just . . ." The warning bell sounded, and I stopped myself from sharing more. "I better get going."

"Just so you know, you don't always have to be *fine*." Tessa patted my shoulder, and I was surprised how comforting the gesture felt.

—ᴍ—

The problem with drama class happening before lunch was that I was always hungry by the time I walked in the door of Ms. Larkin's room. I'd yet to fully relax during the class, and always being hungry—scratch that, definitely hangry—was not doing me any favors. I needed to remember to pack a granola bar or something to scarf down in between classes.

"Shay!"

If I had a dollar for how many times Amelia had yelled my name at school in the past week, I'd have enough to buy a horse.

I waved at her across the room and gratefully deposited my cell phone in the shoe organizer Ms. Larkin kept near the door. No phones in class? No problem. Maybe Ms. Larkin was a Luddite too.

Amelia might be scatterbrained, but she was always early to drama class. And apparently everyone else was too. I was the last of our group to plop into a chair.

"Intercalate," Izzy said.

I swiveled toward her. "What?"

"Word of the day." Izzy puffed up a little. "I'm trying to memorize different words for class."

"But what does it mean?" Amelia said.

Izzy clenched her eyes closed as if trying to jog her memory. "Um . . . to insert something. In a calendar, I think."

"Like our Christmas play!"

Tessa and I both groaned at the same time. *Labradoodle* fit Amelia in more than one way. Sometimes she could be like a dog with a bone. Which reminded me . . . I elbowed Izzy. "My aunt's fostering a dog. A greyhound."

Her eyes lit up. "Oh, my stars!" Her brother Sebastian was allergic, otherwise she'd probably have a menagerie of animals like I would.

Ms. Larkin gave a few claps, and just like that our conversation ceased and class began.

"We're going to talk about the worst moments in our lives."

She said it like it was going to be fun, but I felt myself deflate. *Great.* Today was a "therapy" class. Ms. Larkin was fond of holding "sessions" where we talked about our feelings and how to tap into them for whatever character we were trying to portray. I had a hard-enough time playing my own character in my own life. I didn't need to add a fictional person's drama, pun intended.

Tessa leaned toward me. "Breathe."

"I'm trying."

"Me too."

I guessed what her worst moment would be, but she didn't know mine. Either way, neither of us wanted to talk about it in front of our class.

The first one to share was a guy named Chad, who I considered the male version of Amelia. He was completely gung ho for this stuff like she was. He practically leapt up onto our stage at the edge of the room and talked about moving away from his childhood home when he was ten and struggling to make new friends.

"Good job. Next?" Ms. Larkin seemed to make eye contact with all of us at the same time.

Amelia's hand shot up, and our teacher chuckled, gesturing for her to take the stage. I could already feel my heart pounding at the thought of climbing those two steps, but Amelia took them with confidence and stood center stage, her legs slightly apart, her arms relaxed at her sides.

Amelia's face stilled, and I imagined her pretending she was another famous actress whose name I probably didn't know. She'd told me she always liked to imagine real cameras rolling, capturing her performance for posterity. She glanced off toward the classroom's window with a view of the school's agricultural space, now dormant. I wished the view was of something else. Seeing the field always made me long to be free and out in the open air, cold or not.

I focused on Amelia, wondering if she'd get tapped for being overly dramatic. But Ms. Larkin usually gave us a lot of freedom to express, especially in this format.

"The worst day of my life was when my brother, Josh, got married."

Several kids started to laugh at her statement, but I saw a flash of hurt cross Amelia's face at the reaction. She wasn't trying to be funny.

"My older brother was my best friend," Amelia continued. "We could talk, *really* talk, about pretty much everything. When he and his girlfriend got 'serious—'" air quotation marks around *serious*— "I was devastated."

Amelia's eyes dropped to the stage for a moment.

"What did that look like for you, that devastation?" Ms. Larkin prompted.

"I stayed in my room. I ate a lot of burritos."

The class laughed again, and this time Amelia smiled.

"Josh broke my heart when he left, but I am determined to rise again!" Amelia pumped her fist, and everyone clapped.

I had to hand it to her. She belonged onstage, working a crowd.

Two more girls went, and then it was Izzy's turn. She climbed up onto the stage with less pomp than Amelia but exuding a quiet confidence. "When I was in kindergarten, my class went on a field trip to a corn maze." Izzy's voice seemed so relaxed, and it was easy to settle in for her story. "I got lost, and my teacher couldn't find me. I remember how scared I was at being alone, and I felt panicked to find my way out."

Izzy glanced down at me, and I smiled at her.

"It was a dog who saved me," she said. "He just found me and led me out of that maze to his farm. The farm had a farmer, and he discovered me." Izzy's voice got a little lower. "I was still so scared. But he found my frantic teacher, and everything ended up okay."

When Izzy stepped off the stage, Ms. Larkin called my name. I wanted to hide in the bathroom. Anything but get up on that platform. My mind flipped through the scenarios I could share. Ms. Larkin had to know how much I would hate an exercise of this kind. *Why had she picked this question?* I could "connect" with a character just fine without digging so deep.

I stood up.

"You can do this," Tessa whispered.

I didn't believe her, but I didn't feel I had a choice. All eyes were on me as I crossed the carpet, then the floor, and then made it to the stage stairs. Two steps. That's all they were. But they seemed insurmountable. I really didn't belong here. Not in this class, not even in Riverbend.

But somehow, I made it up to the stage.

"Come closer to the edge," Ms. Larkin advised.

Why couldn't she have picked the *best* moments of our lives? I could manage that. I'd talk about my first time riding a horse and how amazing that felt. Or when my dad and I took that road trip to California when I was twelve. But the worst? I'd had too many of those recently.

I stared out at the class. Most of them actually wanted to be here. They wanted to learn what it took to put on a good stage production and how to become a better actor. Some of them dreamed of having an acting career.

Then there was me. Forced to take the class because of school requirements.

I looked over at Tessa, Amelia, and Izzy. I'd met this trio here, sure. We'd become friends, and I really needed them. Maybe I could focus on that.

"When you're ready, Shay," Ms. Larkin said. "It doesn't have to be long."

Clearing my throat, I let myself remember.

"The worst moment in my life . . ." I swallowed the marble in my throat, trying to push out the truth. This was crazy. I didn't need to bare my soul in front of the class. I could come up with a different bad moment. Like the time I fell off a horse and broke my arm as a kid and had to wait three hours to get to the hospital because my grandmother's cell phone battery ran out and she couldn't call an ambulance. Or the time I got an F on a spelling test and almost flunked English. No one would know any different.

For some reason I glanced down at Tessa again, and when she grinned up at me, I thought of her concern at my locker and how she'd checked in to see if I was okay. I might be able to fool the class and even Izzy and Amelia, but I couldn't seem to fool her. If I fibbed now, she would know. And even if she forgave me for not braving the scrutiny of the class, I would have lied to my friend.

"The worst moment was . . . the day my dad died," I blurted before I could talk myself out of it.

Someone gasped, and I quickly searched Tessa's face for understanding. I found it in her kind smile and hoped she'd also understand why I hadn't first told her or the other girls this huge piece of my story.

I ran my fingers through my hair and focused on the window. Anywhere other than the rest of my classmates.

Silence. They were waiting for me to continue.

But I was done. That was it. The cold hard truth in five words.

Chapter
5

I ATE LUNCH ALONE OUTSIDE. By the time I finished my peanut butter sandwich and McIntosh apple and washed it down with a bottled water, I was nearly frozen. Seemed appropriate. It wasn't like I obsessed over my dad's death every day, but the fact that it had bothered me so much to share even that small morsel proved how close to the surface everything was.

I managed to avoid my friends, and pretty much everyone else, for the rest of the school day. The walk "home" helped a little. I climbed up the outside apartment stairs and let myself inside. Stanley and my aunt weren't anywhere to be found, so I closed myself in my room and tried to read the science fiction novel I'd grabbed out of a box in the storeroom. I got a text a few minutes later from Tessa. It was just three little red hearts, and it calmed down my worries she would be hurt in some way that I hadn't told her about my dad.

I was still in my room when I heard Aunt Laura walk in the door.

"Shay?"

"In here!"

"We brought pizza."

That woke me up. I met my aunt in the kitchen as the scent of pepperoni and cheese wafted out of the pizza box on the counter. Another box held breadsticks. My stomach growled.

Aunt Laura smiled. "How was school?"

I started to shrug, not really wanting to talk about it, but then I reminded myself my aunt was trying. We both had to make concessions every once in a while. I plopped down into a chair and rested my arms and chin on the small kitchen table.

"It was okay," I said.

"Just okay?"

"Drama was tough." I told her about Ms. Larkin's exercise. "I wish I could quit the class."

My aunt poured us water and set out two plates. "That does sound hard, but you'll get through it."

"I just miss Dad so much."

"Me too."

Her response surprised me since my mom had died when I was so young. Before all this, I hadn't really known my aunt outside of Christmas and birthday cards, and I figured she didn't really have reason to contact Dad often.

"Don't look at me like that," Aunt Laura said with a chuckle. "Your father and I talked sometimes. Especially if you ever got ornery and he needed girl advice."

Well, then. News to me.

"Shay, I think it's best if we're completely honest with each other." She pulled a pizza slice from the box and gestured for me to do the same.

I mumbled my agreement as I took a huge bite of the cheesy

goodness. Stanley stood right beside me, staring at the slice in my hand. I studied my aunt while we ate for a moment in silence. She was my mom's younger sister by ten years, which put her in her twenties when Mom had died. It was hard to picture what that experience had been like for my aunt since I had no siblings, but I understood losing someone.

"What do you remember about Mom?"

Aunt Laura finished off her pizza slice and licked her fingers. "She made me laugh."

"Dad always said she had a good sense of humor."

"The best."

"I wish I could've known her."

Laura held up a finger. "She also could be the most stubborn woman in the world."

I smiled. "Maybe it runs in the family."

My aunt laughed.

"Did you fight a lot?"

"Less than you'd think."

"What else?"

"I remember when she told me she was pregnant with you. She told me before anyone else."

"Before her husband?"

My aunt opened the breadstick box, and the garlic and oil scent filled the room. She took one out and offered me another. I got the distinct feeling she was avoiding a response but couldn't figure out why. She took two bites before meeting my eyes, and I noticed the wrinkles around hers.

"I knew you'd ask me these sorts of things at some point. I just didn't expect them so soon."

I wiped my mouth with a napkin. "I do know my dad wasn't my biological father."

"Okay."

"But it didn't matter to me."

"Definitely not, Shay. That's not what I meant." Laura nodded, finishing off her breadstick. "It's just that your mom wasn't married when she got pregnant."

I stopped with my pizza slice halfway to my mouth.

"It wasn't a huge secret, but I didn't know if you knew, or if it was my place to tell you."

No, I hadn't known, and I wasn't sure if that changed anything or not. I tried to remember what my dad had told me. I'd wondered things, but I usually didn't ask since I didn't want to hurt him. He was my father and always would be, blood ties or not.

"They actually never did get married," Aunt Laura said.

Whoa. I set my pizza down. "Were they going to?"

"I think your mom wanted that."

But he didn't? That was the implication here, right? Had she told him about me, and he freaked out? Didn't want to be a father?

"She met your dad when you were six months old. They dated a few months and then got married."

"A few months?"

Aunt Laura smiled. "I know!"

Somehow it hadn't felt comfortable asking Dad about this stuff, but it was easy to talk to my aunt. She was the one bringing it up, and that helped. But I already wasn't liking all the answers. I wasn't shocked, but this definitely threw a wrench in my idealized version of Mom. I had thought she was a Christian ever since she was a kid. And it's not like I assumed Christians were immune to mistakes. We were all on an even playing field when it came to sin, but it was different when it was your mom.

"Did you know my—" I almost said "real" dad, but that didn't seem right—"my biological father?"

A slight nod was my answer. I waited for more. My aunt focused on her plate. Then she carefully lifted another pizza slice from the box, but the strands of mozzarella stretched, not letting her take it.

"I knew him. Not well, but I did."

"What was he like?"

"Do you really want to know?"

"Why wouldn't I?"

"Because once you know things, you can't unknow them."

Okay . . .

"Was he a criminal or something?"

"No, no. Nothing like that."

I knew she was trying to protect me from something, but hinting at stuff like this was like waving a bone in front of a starving dog and then hiding the bone in the refrigerator. What's the dog going to do? Stare at the fridge. Just like I was staring at my aunt. This was a part of me, like it or not. I needed to know where I came from.

"Can you at least tell me his name?"

My aunt blinked. Paused. "John."

Something changed right then. It was one thing to know I had another father out there somewhere, but he'd been like a ghost in my mind. Fleeting and distant, a mist on the outskirts of my life. Nothing solid. Not really human. But put a name to that mist? Instantly he solidified in front of me.

John.

Like the apostle. I pulled my leg up under myself and leaned forward, waiting for my aunt to share more.

"This isn't a good idea."

I'm sure my eyebrows raised. "You can't just tease me like that."

"Greg was your father, Shay. And he was a good one."

"But what if . . . ?"

Yeah, Shay. What if? What am I hoping for here? Not in a million years was I looking to replace Dad. That was impossible. But what if, maybe, I could have another father figure in my life to help me navigate some of the stuff dads do best? Like learning to drive. I'm not sure if I want my aunt to be sitting beside me reminding me of all the dangers I'd encounter. Dads are usually more chill.

My aunt had a point though, and a sliver of guilt poked me. I didn't want to be disloyal. *And what in the world would my grand-parents think?*

"Do you know where he is?"

Aunt Laura wasn't looking me in the eyes anymore. She got up and put her plate in the sink, even though I knew she was still hungry. Sometimes she forgot to eat lunch when she got really busy in the bookstore. Dinner was her favorite meal and one where she actually tried not to eat and run.

Finally, she spun around. "I do, Shay. I'm just not sure I should tell you. Not now at least."

"Why not?"

I could see the conflict in her eyes. *She does care about me, but can she really understand how I feel? I am so tired of people making decisions about me and for me. Couldn't I, just for once, be the one to decide?*

"Can we sleep on it?"

I wanted to press her to tell me, but maybe she was right. I had a lot to digest here, and sometimes things were clearer in the morning.

Chapter
6

But things were *NOT* clearer in the morning.

I reached down and rested my hand on my aunt's cat, Matilda, who'd burrowed in my bed sometime in the night. Her fur was soft under my fingers, and she purred at my touch. It was a good way to wake up.

"Rise and shine," I whispered.

I spent a few minutes staring at the ceiling just stroking Matilda before braving the chilly room. My mind wandered. My first question was, did I trust my aunt? I honestly didn't know a lot about her, so it was hard to base anything on experience. But if my dad had called her for advice, then she had to be trustworthy in some sense. And my grandparents trusted her with *me*, though it also could've been because they had nowhere else to dump me. Either way, my aunt took me in when no one else would. That counted for something. *But why in the world wouldn't she tell me where my bio dad is? She said herself he isn't a criminal.*

The only thing clear to me now was how much I wanted to meet him, good or bad. I could decide where I went after that.

I climbed out of bed. I'd laid my school clothes out the night before and dressed in them so fast I actually scared Matilda because she zipped off the bed. It was normal for me to wake up before my aunt, the night owl, and whoever woke first turned up the heat.

I almost tripped on Stanley who'd camped out in my doorway. He jumped up when he saw me, wagging his tail. I rubbed his ears, and he made a cute groaning sound to indicate his pleasure.

A few minutes later Aunt Laura shuffled into the kitchen yawning, still in her pajamas. I'd already eaten a bowl of Raisin Bran and turned on the coffee maker. It finished sputtering the last drops of dark brew, and my aunt mechanically poured herself a cup.

"You look great," I joked.

"Watch it, kid."

I held up both hands, palms toward her in surrender.

"Coherent sentences come after coffee."

I handed her the bottle of caramel creamer. She topped off her cup and closed her eyes, dramatically taking her first sip, probably to make me laugh. This was one thing I definitely knew. Don't talk to Aunt Laura about anything remotely serious until she was at least halfway finished with her coffee.

"How do you drink that stuff?"

"How don't you?" she mumbled.

"I'm fifteen."

She shook her head. "Twelve when I started."

"And look at you now."

"Hey, aren't you the kid who drinks Earl Grey tea like some English grandmother or something?"

I laughed and let her have the last word.

Stanley stared at his food bowl, and I remembered I was supposed to feed him and Matilda. Maybe when I was done my aunt would be awake enough. I needed to leave for school soon but didn't want to miss the chance to clear the air.

Aunt Laura sat down at the kitchen table. I fed the animals. Stanley took his time eating his kibble nearly one at a time, but Matilda scarfed hers down like it was her last meal. Then she looked up at me and meowed for more, rubbing up against my leg.

"Sorry, girl."

"Stanley needs to be walked before you leave," Aunt Laura said.

Too bad I couldn't take him to school with me. Izzy would be beside herself. I need to have her over to meet him sometime.

"Aunt Laura?"

"Hmm?"

"Last night."

"I'm still very concerned about you getting hurt."

I started to protest, but my aunt silenced me with a grimace. She gripped her mug a little harder than necessary. "I'd never lie to you, Shay. But I did leave something out."

My heart started pounding.

"I realized that if you're old enough to go through what you have, then you're old enough to know."

I stood there frozen. Somehow, I knew this was one of those moments in life you never forget. A moment where everything got branded on your consciousness. The smell of the almost burnt coffee. The *tap, tap, tap* of Stanley's tail against the cabinet as he stared up at me. Matilda's plaintive meow. Even the time 6:12 emblazoned in green on the microwave clock.

"Your bio dad's name *is* John," my aunt said softly. "But he goes by his middle name now."

"Okay . . ." I started to let out my breath in relief. If that was the worst—

"Mason."

It took a good five seconds for her words to register in my brain.

"The other night when you were playing that video . . . I didn't know how to respond because I wasn't sure how much you knew."

"What . . . I don't understand."

Aunt Laura set down her mug. "Mason King."

"The horse trainer?"

"Yes."

"Aunt Laura, what . . . are you saying?"

"I haven't kept up with him, but once in a blue moon I google his name."

It was my turn to sit down. "Are you saying what I think you're saying?"

She nodded.

"He's my *father*?" My voice rose a few decibels.

"Bio father. Your dad will always be Greg Mitchell."

"Are you kidding me?"

Aunt Laura gave me a why-would-I-joke-at-a-time-like-this look.

But it still didn't register.

Does not compute. Does not compute.

This does not compute.

The horse trainer I'd been following on YouTube since I was eleven is my father?

"Did Dad know?"

"That's the thing." Aunt Laura sighed, taking another sip of coffee. "I'm not sure."

"But how could Mom—?"

"Maybe she did tell him, and maybe he was going to tell you." She took a breath. "Maybe he didn't want to know."

I don't remember him ever saying anything when I watched Mason's videos. *Wouldn't he have said something if he'd known?*

I rubbed at my eyes, still barely able to comprehend. She was right. You couldn't *unknow* something like this, and a part of me wished I'd let this sleeping dog lie.

But do I really want to live my life not knowing the truth? Especially about something as important as family?

"Does he know about *me*?"

Aunt Laura shrugged. "I'm not sure about that either."

"Didn't you and Mom talk?"

"It was a difficult time for your mother, and we weren't always close."

I got up, frustrated with the warring thoughts in my head. A huge part of me was ecstatic that the man I'd idolized could actually be someone I could get to know! He could teach me all about horses, and I could travel the country with him and learn everything I'd always wanted to learn. Then I pictured my dad's face. I wanted to be loyal to him. He's the one who'd loved me and been there for me, not Mason King.

Then there was the fear.

What if he did know about me and didn't want anything to do with me?

"We don't have to make any decisions right now," Aunt Laura said. "Okay?"

I could barely get out a reply, but I nodded, slowly taking Stanley's leash off the peg on the wall by the door. I attached it to his collar and took him outside.

Chapter

7

ON THE WALK TO SCHOOL I stuffed my hands into the pockets of my coat and felt the soft rubber of my OtterBox phone case. I flipped the camera to selfie mode and almost started a Snapchat video before I could question myself.

But I chickened out. My friends really didn't need to know about this. After all, I'd just told them about my dad's death and managed to keep my other biggest secret from them this long. I could keep another.

Somehow I managed to get to school without bumping into anything or anyone.

At my locker I felt numb, which scared me.

"Are you okay?"

I startled when Tessa appeared beside me.

"Yeah," I blurted.

"You don't look it."

"Thanks." My tone was sharper than I'd intended.

Tessa stared at me for a second, and for some reason I felt tears flood into my eyes. I quickly blinked them away.

"Sorry," I said.

"Want to talk at lunch?"

"It's okay. I'll be fine."

Then she gave me "the look" she'd given me the other day when she'd told me I didn't have to always be okay.

"I guess maybe," I said softly.

Tessa's boyfriend, Alex, walked by on his way to class and waved at both of us. She smiled, and I was glad to see her happy.

"How are things going with you guys?" I asked, welcoming the diversion.

"Good," Tessa said.

"Is it weird at all?"

"Weird?"

"Going from friends to more than friends?"

I hoped she wouldn't mind the honest question.

"A little at first," Tessa said. "But I don't know that I'd want it any other way. Being friends first feels right."

I knew what she meant, and yet I didn't. I had no experience in the dating world and not even in the guy-friends world. Maybe it was that I found it hard to know if a guy was being genuine. In the short time I'd been here, I'd seen so many of my peers jump into relationships with guys they barely knew, only to have it crash and burn in a matter of weeks or even days.

Of course, I knew there were good guys too, Alex being one of them, but I wasn't really interested in all that. Give me a horse and a dog over a boyfriend any day. At least animals were honest.

I got through my morning classes without worrying too much, and even drama class breezed by. When I walked into the cafeteria and spotted my friends at our usual table, I joined them.

Amelia and Izzy were eating pizza, and Tessa had a chicken Caesar salad. My peanut butter sandwich seemed boring in comparison, but I didn't mind. It was my staple. Once in a while I added some honey to the opposite side of the bread to sweeten things up.

I glanced at Tessa as I sat down, and she smiled. I didn't think she'd push me to talk if I didn't want to, but in some ways, I wanted her to push today. Just because I'd decided not to Snapchat my news didn't mean they shouldn't know about Mason. They could be good sounding boards for what I should do. *Wasn't that what friends did?* I honestly wasn't sure I knew much about friendship either, but these girls were the closest ones I'd ever had, and you had to start somewhere.

"Did you know that kangaroos can't move backward?"

All of us swung toward Amelia. She'd just taken a huge bite of her pepperoni pizza, and the sound she made at our questioning looks might've been a "What?" I couldn't tell through the food.

Amelia swallowed. "I'm serious."

"And your point . . . ?" I said.

"No point. Just fact."

I pulled out my sandwich and tore it in half. I wasn't sure if I would be hungry enough to eat the whole thing. Even in Drama my appetite had been almost nonexistent, which was highly unusual for me. Maybe I should table the idea to talk about my issues. I'd rather hear about everyone else's. It was so much easier to listen than be the one sharing.

"So what's up?" Izzy pointed at me with her fork. She was weird with her pizza and sometimes ate the toppings off first. "You were even quieter than usual today."

"I . . . just . . ."

How to put this? I just found out who my bio father is?
Nope.
My aunt almost lied to me?
Double nope. Paints Aunt Laura in a bad light, and she is a decent person.

I'm feeling completely lost and have no idea what to do?
Much more accurate but a little too vulnerable. Ugh.

I took a bite of peanut butter and bread hoping to buy myself a few more seconds.

"I'd rather talk about you guys," I finally said, deciding not to look at Tessa.

"So . . ." Amelia spoke between pizza bites. "Let's talk about Zac."

"Who?"

"Zac." Amelia said his name in a dramatic, deep, voiceover tone.

Izzy giggled slightly, Tessa pursed her lips, and I didn't have a clue what was going on.

"And . . . he's sitting right . . . over . . ." Amelia started to point in the direction of the robotics team's table, but Izzy grabbed her arm before she could.

"Don't," Izzy hissed but couldn't hide her grin.

Amelia wouldn't let up and poked our mutual friend who was starting to blush. "He's cute, I admit."

"Am I missing something?" I asked.

Amelia nodded. "Izzy has a crush on Zac Lloyd."

"I do not!"

Leaning forward, Tessa set down her fork. "I thought you liked Cody."

Izzy looked mortified at their teasing, but she didn't protest too much, so maybe she appreciated the attention at the same time. I could tell I'd missed a few conversations here and was trying to keep up. I didn't really know Zac—he was a senior—but Izzy's older sister, Claire, knew him somehow. And Cody was Izzy's neighbor. I think. I wasn't really up on anyone's crushes.

"I didn't know you wanted a boyfriend," I said.

Izzy focused on her pizza and shrugged.

Amelia raised her eyebrows at me.

"Cody's just a friend," Izzy said.

"Hey, it's okay to like a guy. I guess." I lowered my voice. "Or to think he's cute."

Izzy tried to hide her smile, but I saw it creeping onto her face again.

"Have you ever liked a guy?" Amelia asked.

It took me a second to realize the question was for me. "What, me?"

"No, the other Shay."

"Have you?" I said.

Amelia waved her pizza crust in the air. "Nope. Not letting you off that easy."

I knew she was teasing me, but I was still feeling pretty raw about my whole dad dilemma and Amelia's doggedness kind of felt like sandpaper on my skin. I knew she wasn't trying to make me or Izzy uncomfortable, but it still felt a little invasive.

Tessa redid her ponytail and started in on her salad again. "There is such a thing as privacy, Amelia."

"Not with friends," Amelia said.

"Especially with friends," Tessa countered.

"What's that supposed to mean?"

I held up my hand. "I'm not trying to be secretive." *At least not on* this *subject.*

"Okay, then spill."

Tessa rolled her eyes.

"I like guys . . . as friends," I said.

"That's not what I mean."

"It's strange to think of them as anything else."

Using her fork as a pointer, Tessa gestured toward Amelia. "There are a lot more important things in life."

"Says the girl with a boyfriend," Amelia said.

"Ms. Larkin is single," I said. "She seems happy."

Amelia sighed. "But she's *old*."

I leaned forward. "And she's *happy*."

"Guys." Izzy shook her head. "What is with you? Just relax."

Yeah, good question. I was not a fan of arguments, especially with friends, and I didn't even know what we were arguing about.

"Why do we say, 'guys' when we're a bunch of girls?" Amelia asked.

Izzy let out an exasperated sound and pulled out her phone. She held it up and pushed a button, training it on each of us. She loved taking videos at random times to add to her Instagram stories.

"I think it's time for some bonhomie," Izzy said. "What do you say?"

"Some what?" I knew what the word *bonhomie* implied but had no idea its exact meaning. This sounded like another word-of-the-day lesson that Izzy seemed to be enjoying lately.

"Why, I'm glad you asked!" Izzy swung her phone toward me. "*Bonhomie* means good-natured, easy friendliness."

Tessa chuckled. Then we all joined in.

It felt good to laugh, but by the time lunch ended and I was headed to my next class, the feeling of unease that followed me to school sank back down over my shoulders.

Chapter

8

KELSEY AND JADE ambushed me at the door as I was leaving school.

"Where's the fire?"

I was not up for this. I just wanted to get home and read a book or snuggle with Stanley and Matilda and maybe pretend I could actually unknow the Mason King deal.

"School's out. I'm going home." I leaned against the door's exit bar.

Kelsey grabbed my arm.

I pulled away. "Hey."

"See? What'd I tell you?" Kelsey nodded toward Jade, who bobbed her head in response.

Breathe in, breathe out. I tried to calm myself. They were looking for a reaction, most definitely. If I didn't give it to them, maybe they'd leave me alone.

"Your pic was really popular," Jade said.

"What pic?"

"The one I took of you, goof."

In the mouths of my friends, the use of *goof* might've been endearing. On Jade's lips, it was an insult.

"Want to hear some of the comments?"

"Not really."

Jade yanked out her phone, scrolling with her thumb. "*Plain Jane moves to the big city . . . when you look more like your horse than yourself . . .*"

Kelsey laughed much louder than necessary. "Read my fave from Ross."

Jade continued. "*If she was cuter, I'd book a room!!!*"

I almost ripped the phone out of her hands.

"What?" Kelsey let out another laugh. "It's funny!"

Warmth rose up my neck at his crude comment. If I showed my feelings, they'd jab me even more. I was better off walking away, as hard as that was.

"Before you run off, I think we need to talk." Jade stuffed her phone in the back pocket of her tight, rhinestone-studded jeans.

I could feel tension pulling at my insides like a knot. Other students poured past us out the doors. Someone bumped into me then apologized, but I barely noticed. Kelsey pulled me over to the wall, and I wasn't sure why, but I let her.

"I don't want to talk," I said.

"And I get that," Kelsey said. "But this is important."

If she was cuter . . .

I was not the type of girl to worry much about glamour. I'd worn makeup twice in my life, and even then, it was just a little mascara and lipstick. But girly girl or not, the comments still hurt. I didn't want to look pretty for any guy in particular, but I wouldn't have minded if someone thought I was.

"So, here's the thing," Kelsey whispered, leaning in.

I felt myself recoil at how close she was. I could smell her peppermint gum.

"We've heard some rumors." Kelsey glanced at Jade. One side of her mouth turned up into a smirk.

Rumors?

"I really need to get home," I said.

Kelsey crossed her arms. "Calling it home already? Wow, you're adjusting well. Don't think I'd adapt to such a drastic change that quickly."

Is this how Stanley felt when my aunt first brought him to live with her? Because I was starting to feel like a cornered dog.

"Wanna know what they are?" Kelsey elbowed Jade. "Specifics don't really matter, but let's just say your school file has some interesting details."

My pulse pounded faster. I didn't know how much the school knew about me, but I imagine my aunt had to give them *some* details. *Or was it my grandparents?* I wasn't even sure who'd enrolled me here.

"So what?" I said. *And how in the world would they have gathered this supposed information? Hacked into the school's computer? Snuck into an office and pulled my records?*

"You didn't start with the rest of us," Kelsey said. "In fact, you were two weeks late."

"Anyone with eyes could figure that out."

Jade got closer to me and whispered, "But we know why."

"You don't know anything," I said, hoping my statement sounded more confident than I felt.

"Really?"

It was all I could do not to shove my way past them.

Kelsey laughed. "Don't look so scared, Shay."

Is it possible they really did have something on me?

"At least we know she can't go home crying to her daddy," Jade said, and they both laughed together.

I could feel my fingers wanting to ball together into a fist. *How did the news about my dad travel so quickly?* I needed to pretend none of their words mattered to me. That I didn't care. Maybe then they'd leave me alone. Bullies bullied people who reacted.

"Relax. We haven't told anyone."

But what if they did? I could already feel the stares in the hallway just from being the new girl, but the whispers behind my back would become unbearable. The names I'd be called. *What about Amelia, Tessa, and Izzy? Would they even want to be friends with me if they knew?* To them I was the quiet one. The girl who couldn't even raise her voice in drama class. That impression would change—completely.

Jade jovially punched me in the arm. "Maybe there's a way you can help us. We'll let ya know, okay?"

They started to walk away.

"What are you talking about?" I asked.

"Later," Kelsey said with a backward wave.

I watched them disappear out the school doors. Once outside they gave each other a high five, hooked arms, and practically skipped away, laughing.

I waited until they were gone before I slammed into the exit bar with a lot more force than needed and began my walk home. I could feel the anger burning hot in me now, that fire I couldn't always quench but knew I should. At least the chilly air would help clear my mind.

But before I could cross the parking lot, Tessa came up beside me and wrapped her arm around my shoulder, steering me toward her boyfriend's car.

"Let me and Alex drive you home. He gave me his keys so we can wait where it's warm."

"I'm fine."

Tessa unlocked the car with her key fob. It chirped. "Shay, stop. For once let someone do something for you. It's freezing."

I nodded without arguing and got in the passenger seat, setting my backpack in between my feet. I don't know if she realized how much I needed and appreciated people pushing me to accept care. I couldn't seem to allow it on my own, and I wasn't even sure why.

Tessa hopped into the driver's seat. She started the engine and the heater.

"Were those girls bothering you?"

I stared at the floor. "What girls?"

"They were kind of cornering you."

Has she been watching the whole time? What has she heard?

"I can handle it," I said.

Tessa leaned back into her seat, holding the steering wheel with both hands. I was getting the vibe she wasn't happy with me. I definitely enjoyed all of my friends, but Tessa seemed to understand me a little better than the others. She could go deep, too, which I loved. Disappointing her was the last thing I wanted, and it wasn't something I could emotionally deal with right now.

An uncomfortable moment of silence spread through the car. I wanted to fill it, but I was still shaken from my encounter with Kelsey and Jade.

"I'm just trying to help," Tessa said.

I swallowed. "Thank you."

"Why didn't you talk at lunch? I thought you wanted to."

I shrugged.

"But there's definitely something going on, right?"

You could say that. But even with her genuine concern, I felt myself clam up.

"Shay."

"It's about my dad."

"Okay."

"I'm sorry I didn't tell you about him sooner."

"Hey, I get it. Stuff like that's hard to talk about."

"Ms. Larkin caught me off guard."

Tessa chuckled. "She has a way of doing that."

I sighed, thankful to clear the air because I had more to say. "There's something else. I knew I was adopted. I've always known, but . . ." *Why is this so hard? Mason King is my father! Shouldn't I be shouting it from the rooftops? He's a celebrity in the horse world.*

"What is it?"

"Last night my aunt told me who my bio father is."

Tessa's eyes widened.

"And it turns out he's . . ." I twisted in my seat to face her. "Remember that horse trainer I was telling you about? The one I wished I could go see?"

She nodded.

"Him."

"You're kidding."

"I'm not."

"Shay, that's . . ."

"Crazy?"

Tessa grinned. "Wow."

"I have no idea how I feel about it."

"That's definitely a lot to take in."

"Tell me something I don't know."

"But it's exciting too?"

"I guess . . . a little."

"I can see why the middle of the cafeteria might not have been the best place to tell the girls."

I managed a smile.

"So . . . what's next?"

I explained what Aunt Laura said, and Tessa listened.

"What would *you* do?" I asked.

Tessa tapped the steering wheel and adjusted the heater to blow more warm air on us. I wondered if she was thinking about her own father, who'd recently left her mom for another woman, his former girlfriend. Parents sure were complicated.

"I think it's different if your adoptive dad's not here," Tessa said. "If you found this out when he was still alive, it could be harder. Not that it's easy now."

"Is it wrong that I want to meet him?"

Tessa's eyes softened, and she touched my arm. "Why would it be?"

"I would be betraying Dad."

"No, you're not."

"I'd be comparing them." Dad was the artistic, designer type. Mason was an outdoorsy horseman. I guess I had bits of both of them in me.

"Which would be completely normal." Tessa pulled her dark-brown hair out from its rubber band and let it fall to her shoulders. I don't think she realized how pretty she was. No-nonsense and athletic, swim team had muscled her frame, and she could somehow wear makeup without looking like she did.

"Maybe your aunt will come around," Tessa said. "Or maybe it's for the best to just let it go."

"Ha!" I threw myself back into my seat. "Like that's gonna happen."

"Well, then at least you know what you want."

Do I?

She had a point. If I couldn't let it go, then that meant I wanted to see him. But that also meant convincing my aunt to let me, which might be like convincing Stanley to stop chasing squirrels.

But there was something else I felt inside me, something I couldn't quite figure out or verbalize. It was this gnawing sensation that hid behind me and kept me from fully embracing the excitement.

When Alex joined us a few minutes later, I was still trying to figure it out.

Chapter
9

I SPENT THE REST OF THE DAY helping my aunt restock shelves, and later we had pizza again and watched an episode of a superhero show Aunt Laura enjoyed. Neither of us brought up last night's and this morning's conversations. I didn't because I didn't want to hear my aunt tell me I couldn't see my bio dad, and maybe she didn't because she didn't want to tell me. Probably both of us needed to digest the implications of it all. I tried to act like nothing was wrong, but when I closed myself in my bedroom at eight o'clock, I couldn't shake my anxiety.

I slipped out my phone and started a text to my friends in our group chat. They deserved to know, even though Tessa already did. It took me ten minutes to craft just the right words, but I decided it was the right thing to do.

> Sorry if I was weird at lunch today. I wanted to tell you guys something but didn't know how. I

just found out who my biological father is, and I'm freaking out. He's a horse trainer named Mason King.

In less than thirty seconds, my friends began responding.

Amelia: Oh my gosh!!! 😳 🐴
Izzy: Whoa! Really?!?!?!

I quickly sent them a link to my favorite YouTube video of Mason, the one where he had this little paint mustang in a round pen, and before the session is over, she's following him around like a puppy. My favorites were always the ones where he worked with the wild mustangs. I wouldn't have been surprised if he was ever invited to Road to the Horse, a wild horse–gentling competition.

Amelia: He looks so cool!!

I smiled at her response; glad someone saw him in a positive light.

Tessa: How are you holding up?

I hesitated to respond back to that one. I wanted to be honest, but it was hard to share my feelings with anyone, much less these girls I'd only known for a couple of months. But Tessa had shown she cared today, so she deserved a real answer.

Me: Pretty nervous. ☺
Amelia: Nervous???
Izzy: I totally would be too!

Really? That makes me feel better.

Tessa: What are you nervous about?

Tessa had this thing about using correct grammar and no abbreviations in her texts. I didn't have to see her profile pic beside her words to know they were from her.

I started to tap out a response but then deleted it. Then started again but deleted that too. Finally, I tapped out: Not sure what to do. Want to meet him. Aunt doesn't agree.

> Amelia: I want to meet him too!

I smiled.

> Tessa: Does your aunt have a reason?
> Me: She doesn't like him.
> Izzy: Why not?

Good question.

> Me: Not sure. Thinks he's a con artist?
> Amelia: She watched the videos?
> Me: Yes.
> Tessa: Where does he live?

Another very good question. I was pretty sure it was Texas, but I did a quick Google search and found Mason's website. It was tasteful and had some awesome photos of horses he'd trained. On the About page I found his official headshot. He was dressed in jeans and a denim shirt, and his black cowboy hat sat low on his head. A couple days' worth of stubble covered his chin, and he stared at the camera with a crooked grin that made me smile too. *Wow. A real cowboy. I can't believe I'm his daughter!*

I actually started to get excited when I clicked through the site and read all about how he'd been working with horses since he was a boy and saved up his money to buy his own when he was ten. His parents supported him, even when he quit school to apprentice for an old-time cowboy out West. That's when it hit me. *Parents.* That meant I had another set of grandparents.

I downloaded the photo from his site and sent it to my friends. Amelia sent back five hearts, a cowboy hat, and several more horse emojis.

> Izzy: He looks like a movie star! You have his eyes!

I stared at the photo. *I did?*

> Tessa: I can see the resemblance too. But you're much prettier!

Her comment warmed me and helped to counter the comments Jade and Kelsey zinged at me earlier. I wondered if I should tell my friends about that too. Maybe later.

> Me: Makes me want to ride again so much.
> Tessa: What's keeping you from it?
> Me: $$$. A horse. LOL
> Tessa: There's a stable not too far from my house.
> Me: What???
> Izzy: She's right. I forgot. It's small, but you should go see it!
> Amelia: I'M IN!!!
> Me: What if he doesn't know about me?
> Izzy: Any father would be proud to have you as his daughter.
> Me: Aw, thanks!
> Tessa: Definitely true.

My eyes started to fill up at their kindness.

> Amelia: ❤❤❤❤❤
> Me: But really, what if?
> Tessa: You should ask your aunt.
> Me: Did. She doesn't know.

Izzy: Hmm . . . maybe he does know about you?

I wasn't sure if that would be any easier. *If he knew about me, then why hadn't he contacted me? Had my father or mother told him not to? If so, why? If not, then did that mean he didn't care about me?* My thumbs hovered over the phone. I took a deep breath. Typed. Hit Send before I could take it back.

Me: I don't want to disappoint him.

There. I said it.

Amelia: Won't know until you meet him!
Me: So you think I should?
Izzy: Pray about it?

A bucketful of guilt poured over me. I hadn't brought any of this to God. Hadn't even thought about it. I'd been a Christian since I was little, and Dad taught me right and wrong from the Bible. We weren't as faithful at going to church as my grandparents wanted us to be, but we tried. I think maybe it was hard for my father, being a single dad. Churches didn't always understand us. Single moms, yes. Help them all you can. Provide whatever they need. Single dads? Not so much.

Me: I forgot to pray. I hope God understands.
Izzy: Of course He does!
Tessa: Don't beat yourself up. We all mess up on this.
Amelia: What's the verse in James? About wisdom?
Izzy: James 1:5

I knew which one she was talking about but didn't have it memorized.

Izzy: Just grabbed it from Bible Gateway! "If any of you lacks wisdom, let him ask God."

> Amelia: Him or her!
> Izzy: LOL
> Me: Thank you.
> Izzy: "Who gives generously to all without reproach."

It was always a hard concept for me: God actually forgiving and loving us, even when we make mistakes. I knew it was real and believed it in my heart, but in the practical, everyday life it was harder to understand. School hadn't helped me with that either. I was surrounded now every day by kids whose ideals clashed with mine. Sure, there were some Christians, like my friends, but we also had kids who hated God and weren't afraid to say it or mock those who believed.

> Tessa: You'll know what to do, Shay.
> Me: I hope so.
> Izzy: Let's pray now.
> Amelia: 👍
> Tessa: Yes.
> Izzy: Father, we ask You to help Shay. Show her what to do. Give her wisdom. Let her know You'll always be there for her and always have been. Amen.

I felt those stupid tears again, and in the privacy of my bedroom I let them fall. They weren't tears of sadness. I cried from the kindness of my friends, and I wondered if they had any idea how much I needed that.

> Me: You guys are great.
> Amelia: LOVE YOU ALL!! ❤❤❤
> Tessa: Good night. See you tomorrow.
> Izzy: Buenos noches!!!

Before I went to sleep, I binge-watched Mason King YouTube videos. I left my door open, and sometime in the night both Stanley and Matilda snuggled up to me. For the first time since arriving, I slept soundly.

Chapter
10

WHEN I WOKE UP THE NEXT MORNING, I felt a peace I hadn't felt in a long time. The texting conversation with my friends was still fresh in my mind, and I had a warm kitty and dog curled up against me. For some reason the heater was on too. Aunt Laura must've gotten up early. My phone pulsed again beside me, and I fumbled for it, groggily swiping the screen to silence the alarm I'd snoozed twice already.

Aunt Laura was finishing a cup of coffee when I walked into the kitchen. She pointed at a steaming cup of Earl Grey tea on the counter she must've made for me. *Wow. That was sweet.*

"Cereal's on the table," Aunt Laura said.

I mumbled my thanks and sat down, pouring myself half a bowl of Raisin Bran and drenching it with 2% milk.

"Your grandparents are coming for dinner tonight."

With that one sentence my peace flew out the door like a racehorse at the starting gate.

I tried not to choke on a bran flake. "What?"

"Can you do a little straightening up when you get home from school?" Aunt Laura said as she topped off her mug with more from the pot.

"Tonight?"

"I kinda didn't want to tell them no," my aunt said with a sympathetic wince. "It could be a good thing."

"Give me one reason." I shoved a bite of cereal in my mouth. I didn't want to sound like a snotty teenager since my aunt was already dealing with enough from me, but I was not prepared for talking with my grandmother. I needed time to decompress. To sink into a routine.

"They care about you."

I had no response to that. *If they care, why pawn me off?*

"In their own way, they really do."

"Doesn't feel like it."

"I know." My aunt leaned against the counter, sipping her coffee with one hand, petting Stanley's head with the other.

"How'd you end up with Stanley?"

"Whoa. Change of topic much?"

"I didn't realize you liked dogs."

"Oh my gosh, yes." She waved her hand to indicate the apartment. "Just never had a lot of room or time, but I grew up with them. Where do you think you got your love of animals?"

"My dad?"

"Him too, but your mom and I had pets for as long as I can remember." My aunt grinned and confessed, "We even had a pet snake once."

I grimaced. "Ew."

"Your mom couldn't handle feeding it live mice, so we gave him to a neighbor boy."

I pointed at the dog. "You should adopt him."

Aunt Laura glanced down at Stanley, who was leaning against her leg. Apparently it was a greyhound thing. "I think this guy needs a family." She said the words, and then quickly seemed to catch herself. "Not that you and I don't make a family, but—"

"No, I get it."

I did, but sometimes people said things from their heart without thinking first. My aunt had lived a single person's life for all of her thirty-plus years, and she, like Ms. Larkin, was happy. But she was right, too. There was something about a *family*, about surrounding yourself with people who shared your bloodline. They might drive you crazy, but you were connected in some inescapable way.

Then I thought about my dad. He and I weren't connected in that way at all, and yet I'd loved him as if we were. *I know he loved me, too, but was it possible he would've loved me more if he'd been my biological father? How could you measure something like that?*

"Shay, you know that's not what I meant."

"Mm-hmm." I shoveled Raisin Bran in my mouth and just focused on eating and getting out the door.

"I have a book sale I'm going to around noon, but I'll be back before they arrive." Aunt Laura said as she grabbed Stanley's leash. "I can walk him."

She left, and I wondered if it was because she was embarrassed or didn't know what to say any more than I did. I finished my cereal as I scrolled through last night's messages from my friends. Amelia had already sent us all a Snapchat video this morning. I clicked on it.

"Hey there . . ." she waved at the camera. "So . . . have we made up our minds about the Christmas play? I *really* think we need to do it. It could be soooo much fun. See ya at school!"

I gave Matilda the stink eye. Amelia just wouldn't let it go. Her stick-to-itiveness both annoyed and challenged me. I wished I could be as excited about something, anything really, because I certainly wasn't excited about school.

"Hold down the fort," I admonished the cat and ran out the door.

———m———

Thankfully Jade and Kelsey weren't waiting for me when I arrived at school, but Izzy was. She handed me a baggie with two brownies in it.

I think my eyes lit up. "Wow, thanks."

"I thought they might help."

When Izzy made brownies, they weren't just brownies. They were usually from scratch and sometimes loaded with chocolate chunks or decorated with cute sprinkles.

"I added some white chocolate chips," Izzy said.

"You have to share these with me at lunch."

She waved me off. "I ate way too many last night!"

That's one of the things I loved about her. She wasn't afraid to enjoy food. I wasn't sure if it was part of her Mexican heritage or just her, but food was both how she showed care and how she brought a certain zest to her life.

"You should start a YouTube cooking channel," I said. Izzy dreamed of someday having her own baking show on Netflix.

"That's soooo been done."

"Not by you."

She playfully punched my arm. "We're gonna be late."

"Ugh, 'cause I'm so excited to learn about empires of Asia."

"Hey, that Ming Dynasty keeps me up at night."

We both laughed.

Tessa and I had second-hour Chemistry together, but I didn't get to talk to her. I didn't see any of my other friends until drama class. They all converged around me like I was a flower and they were a swarm of bees.

Amelia wrapped me in one of her infamous hugs. "I watched five of his videos last night. How in the world does he do all that?"

"He is pretty cool, isn't he?"

"Did you talk to your aunt again?" Tessa asked.

"No."

Tessa's forehead scrunched up. "You really should."

"I will. Just not now."

"Shay, you can't put everything off."

I felt myself bristle. I didn't put *everything* off. I knew Tessa was trying to help though, so I let the comment slide.

Ms. Larkin stood up, and we all sat down and got quiet.

"Today we're going to play a game called 'Anyone Like Me?'"

Amelia elbowed Izzy in excitement as if she knew what was coming.

Ms. Larkin directed us to arrange the chairs (and beanbags) in a circle around the huge pink chair shaped like a high-heeled shoe.

"I'll start so you get the idea," she said. "I'm looking for people who, like me, love the color purple. Anyone who is like me, please stand up."

Five kids, including Amelia, stood.

"That's great! Now all of us standing will change seats."

There was a fun scramble around the room, and Amelia ended up in the center chair.

"Okay, Amelia, your turn. Who are you looking for?"

She thought for one second and then blurted, "I'm looking for people who, like me, have math as their worst subject in school!"

I groaned and stood up with several others. We switched seats, and I ended up sitting next to Tessa.

Chad was in the hot seat now. "I'm looking for people who, like me, wish drama class was two hours long!"

Everyone stood up except me and Tessa, and we looked at each other sheepishly as a few of the kids pointed at us. I knew it was all in fun, but I didn't enjoy the way it made me feel like an outsider.

"Okay, this is great," Ms. Larkin said. "But let's think about going deeper, all right? Don't be afraid to delve into some unknowns. You're safe here."

When Izzy got up, she said, "I'm looking for people who, like me, love to watch *Cupcake Wars*."

Only two students stood up with her, including Ms. Larkin.

Ms. Larkin ended up in the middle. "I'm looking for people who, like me, sometimes feel lonely."

I almost didn't stand up, but I finally did. I looked around the room and was surprised that a bunch of kids, including all three of my friends, had joined me. *Really? How could vivacious Amelia ever feel like that, or Izzy, with her amazing cooking and baking skills and always trying to cheer others up. And Tessa always seemed so put together and kind. Lonely? I'd never thought of her that way either.*

And then I was standing in the middle.

I wasn't as uncomfortable as I had been on the stage, but once again I felt the panic of having all eyes on me. I knew everyone here wanted to be supportive, but that didn't really help.

"I'm looking for people who, like me—" I struggled to pick something that wasn't entirely superficial but wasn't all that vulnerable either—"love animals."

Okay, that was safe. A half dozen students stood, including Izzy.

Two rounds later Tessa stood up in the center. She blinked a few times and glanced up at the ceiling like she was contemplating what to say. "I'm looking for people who, like me . . ."

She paused, and I wondered if she was having a similar debate with herself about how deep to go.

". . . who, like me, have parents who are getting divorced."

I watched as four other students stood with her, and it almost seemed like Tessa's shoulders relaxed at the confirmation she wasn't alone. I think we all were aware of her parents' situation, but I knew admitting that up in front of the class took some guts.

In a few more minutes I found myself in the hot seat again after standing because Izzy asked who else loved pizza. I'd relaxed a little, and I almost went for another superficial share. But if Tessa had been brave enough, I could be too.

"I'm looking for people who, like me, have had a parent die."

The class became still. Someone's sneaker squeaked on the floor. Chad tapped a pen on his leg.

No one stood.

I felt my heart ramping up, and I wished there was such a thing as an invisibility cloak. I would've thrown it over my head in a heartbeat.

Ms. Larkin started clapping. "Give Shay a round of applause. It isn't easy being unique and standing up there alone."

I knew she meant it as positive affirmation, and that was the point of this game: to support each other. But I felt the opposite. I didn't want to be singled out. I didn't want to be unique. I wanted someone else to understand me.

Didn't look like that was happening today.

Chapter
11

I LUMBERED UP THE STAIRS outside my aunt's apartment—I didn't know if I'd ever call it mine—and Stanley met me at the door. I wasn't sure how long it had been since he'd done his business, so I quickly walked him before I got to work "straightening" the place like my aunt wanted.

I'm not the neatest person in the world. I probably drove my aunt crazy when I left out a dish or glass in the living room. I could stack a pile of books on my nightstand without even thinking, and sometimes I left dirty clothes on the floor.

My aunt wasn't what you'd call a neat freak either, but she definitely liked things in their place. So I spent a half hour picking up unnecessary clutter with Matilda following me the entire time.

Six o'clock was when dinner was supposed to happen, and by five thirty I could feel my gut tightening with the tension of expectation. *Where was my aunt?* I almost headed downstairs to search for her in the bookstore, but she'd said she was going to a book sale.

I grabbed my phone and punched out a text: Where are you? It's almost 6.

Aunt Laura was *not* a Luddite, but she also sometimes left her phone in her car. She was trying to get better about that for my sake, but old habits die hard. I imagined her phone vibrating in the cupholder of her Jeep.

I decided to feed Stanley and Matilda before my grandparents arrived so the animals would be on their best behavior. I was just picking up their bowls when the knock came at the door.

Running over to answer it, I forgot to check the peephole and swung the door open. My grandparents both visibly startled and then stood staring at me. Grams carried a gift bag with the neck of what had to be a wine bottle poking out the top. My grandfather, who insisted on being called Pawpaw, smiled at me through his bushy white mustache.

I stepped aside and let them in, inwardly yelling for my aunt to hurry up and get home! Stanley greeted them both with a friendly tail wag and sniff to their hands. They both patted him on the head.

Grams reached to give me a hug, but her hugs weren't at all like Amelia's. My grandmother was as thin as a great blue heron's legs, and only her arms touched me for two seconds tops.

"How are you?" she asked.

She hadn't called me or texted or reached out in any way since leaving me here, so it was hard to feel like it was a genuine question. But I knew it was possible she was simply giving me time and space to settle in.

I put on a happy face. "Good."

Grams lifted the wine from the bag, two bottles actually, and placed both on the kitchen table I had yet to set for the meal. I clenched my jaw at her assumption that first of all my aunt would even want to serve alcohol with the food, and then at how she could possibly think it was okay after what happened with Dad.

I glanced at my grandfather, and he shrugged.

Without asking, Grams started opening kitchen drawers. Silverware rattled. I noticed Matilda had disappeared, which was quite unlike her. We sometimes had to close her in a bedroom because she'd be trying to steal the food right off our plates.

"What are you looking for?" I asked.

"Does your aunt have a wine bottle opener?"

"You're opening them now?"

"Red wine needs to breathe."

No, I didn't know where my aunt kept a bottle opener, or if she even had one. I couldn't remember if I'd ever seen her drink anything stronger than her coffee. Maybe she did when I wasn't around or before I came to live with her. I didn't know that either, and it wasn't really my business.

But this? This is.

"Any ideas?" Grams rifled through the knife drawer.

My grandfather sat down at the kitchen table. "Honey, maybe you should wait for Laura."

Grams didn't seem to hear him. She finally found what she was looking for and held the corkscrew up in triumph.

"Who stores this with the measuring cups?" she asked with a laugh. "Shay, can you grab us some wine glasses?"

"I think we should wait too."

My words seemed to fall on my grandmother's deaf ears, though I know she could hear perfectly. I couldn't think of what to say as I watched her find three glasses and open the wine bottle. She poured herself half a glass and took a sip.

"Mmm . . . good choice," she said.

That did it. I picked up my phone and zapped Aunt Laura another text.

Help! They're here!

This time my aunt responded: **On my way!! Sorry!**

I couldn't tell if she was exasperated, sympathetic, or something else.

"So how's school?" My grandfather might've sensed my discomfort, and as usual, he tried to smooth things over with small talk.

"Fine," I said.

"Make any new friends?"

I nodded.

"What are their names?"

I crossed my arms. "Pawpaw, I don't really want to talk about it."

"See?" My grandmother waved a hand toward me, holding her glass in the other. "That right there is exactly what I was talking about, Greg."

My grandfather's name was also Greg. Same as my father's.

"She's still playing the same games."

"I'm not playing games."

My grandmother faced me. She wore a silky white blouse with decorative stitching along the buttons. A delicate gold necklace hung from her neck and rested on freckled skin.

"You're too sensitive, Shay. Your grandfather was just trying to be nice, but could you answer his simple question?"

"I just didn't want to talk about—"

"You never want to talk about anything!" Grams sipped her wine, and I wondered why she was doing this here and now. "We ask you how your day was, you say fine. We ask what you want for dinner, you say you don't care. What are we supposed to do with that?" Grams's voice was rising. "We gave you everything we had, and you thanked us by . . . How could you have done this to us, Shay? After all that we've done for you?"

Whenever I got upset, my eyes seemed to have a will of their own. No matter how hard I tried, tears would come. I tried to blink them away, then opened wider hoping to stop them, but they still filled my eyes.

"I'm sorry," I whispered.

"That's why you're here, you know," Grams said. "Because I can't deal with your attitude anymore."

"Honey . . ." My grandfather's voice was almost a whisper.

"No, Greg. She needs to hear this."

"I think she already has."

"Really?"

My grandparents stared each other down. I knew they were hurting far more than either of them probably realized, but I was too. I swiped at my eyes with the back of my hand.

That's when the apartment door opened, and Aunt Laura waltzed in. "Hi, everyone!"

Feigned smiles slipped onto my grandparents' faces, and they greeted my aunt. She looked at me, and I saw the moment she realized I was upset, given the slight wrinkling of her brow.

"Shay, why don't you take these and then walk Stanley, okay?" Aunt Laura handed me two paper bags with the logo of the Italian restaurant a few blocks away. I was starving, but I wasn't sure if I could eat right now.

I took the bags and set them on the counter, grabbing Stanley's leash off the wall peg. Outside, I didn't care if the cold made me shiver or if I ever went back in there. I let a few tears fall and walked the greyhound in the small grassy area that was my aunt's backyard. Then I sat on the bottom step of the apartment's stairs and rested my head in my hands.

Could I stay out here the whole time they visited?

I knew I couldn't, but I entertained the idea of hanging out in the bookstore for at least an hour. Instead, I pulled out my phone and contemplated texting or Snapchatting my friends.

I finally texted Tessa.

Grandparents over for dinner. Not going well. ☹

It took a minute, but she texted back: **Aw, so sorry! I'll pray.**

My tears returned at her words. It was silly, really. But in that moment knowing my friend was praying for me meant more than she probably realized. I glanced back up at the apartment. My grandparents were Christians, but I knew their son's death had shaken their faith to the core. I once heard a preacher say storms either strengthened your faith or tore it down entirely, and my grandmother's faith especially seemed to have deteriorated. God was the One who knew her heart, but she never used to drink either. And it scared me to see her do it now so openly.

I held my phone and stared at the text thread. *Should I tell her more?* I wasn't sure what the rules of newish friendships were in situations like this.

I finally typed: Grandmother brought wine. Makes me uncomfortable.

> Tessa: Why is that?
> Me: She never used to drink.
> Tessa: That's upsetting.

I hesitated to share more, but I needed to get it off my chest. I typed: A drunk driver caused the accident that killed my dad.

Tessa never used emojis, but her response was a crying face.

It'll be okay, I tapped.

> Tessa: Talk more later? I just got to my swim meet.
> Me: Yes. Have fun.

I put away my phone and climbed back up the stairs before Stanley could start shivering. Just a micro connection with a friend who cared gave me enough energy to dry my tears and walk back inside.

The table was set, and a steaming pan of lasagna sat on the table along with a loaf of garlic bread and tossed salad. That was something I was discovering about my aunt. Garlic, bread, and butter. They were staples in her kitchen.

"Hungry?" Aunt Laura asked when I sat down, but I could see the question in her eyes of whether I was okay or not.

I nodded and gave her a real smile. "Starving."

My grandparents seemed to have settled down, and when we all were finally sitting together, my grandfather bowed his head, ready to pray. "Shall we say grace?"

I closed my eyes.

"Thank You, Lord, for this food," he said. "May You bless it as well as our time together here. In Your name we pray. Amen."

I echoed him and accepted my aunt's offering of a huge slice of the meat sauce lasagna dripping with mozzarella. Stanley rested beside me, his dark eyes watching for any signs of a dropped morsel. Aunt Laura had made it clear he wasn't supposed to have people food or to be rewarded for begging. His new family might not like it.

"So how's the business?" My grandfather began.

For the next few minutes my aunt carried the conversation, sharing about the bookstore and how she wanted to bring in local music acts and maybe even an official coffee bar to the place. I knew a few of the kids at school had started a band. I wondered if they'd want to come and perform here. It might give me some points in the popularity contest to be the owner's niece. Not that I cared too much about being popular, but maybe girls like Kelsey and Jade would leave me alone if I had some of that clout.

"Is Shay staying out of trouble?"

Surprise. My grandmother couldn't seem to get off the subject of my being a burden.

Aunt Laura smiled. "She's been great."

"I imagine it's quite the adjustment having a child in the house."

My aunt cocked her head. "Florence, I don't mean to be rude, but Shay's a good kid. We've all had to make adjustments, her included. But we're making it work."

I stared into my lasagna and felt my heart warm toward my aunt.

"I'm not sure about the *good* part these days, but I do hear what—"

"Excuse me?" Aunt Laura said as she set down her fork.

"I think you heard me, Laura."

My aunt glared at Grams for a second. "And I think maybe we need to change the subject here because I'm not liking where this is going."

"The truth isn't always easy to hear."

"Agreed," Aunt Laura said.

"Guys, I'm right here." I pushed my plate toward the center of the table.

"Okay, look. Let's all just take a deep breath." My aunt sipped from her water glass. "We're family. Let's remember that."

Grams reached for the wine bottle and refilled her glass. She didn't ask my grandfather but went ahead and refilled his, too. "Not to be nitpicky, but technically, that's not entirely true."

Her words hit me like ice water in the face. For a second I thought she was talking about my aunt, who wasn't related to either of them. That would've been bad enough. But no. She was talking about me. Her son had been my father through adoption, not blood.

My aunt stared at my grandmother in disbelief and then shook her head. "I can't believe you just said that."

"Don't get me wrong; we're happy to be grandparents, but . . ."

"But what?"

Pawpaw, who'd remained quiet, as usual, for most of the conversation, placed his hand on his wife's arm.

She didn't seem to notice. "It explains things is all I'm saying."

"And what exactly does it explain, Florence?"

It was weird to hear my grandmother's first name. I'm not sure if it was a good thing or not that my aunt wasn't letting this go.

Do I really want to hear what my grandmother has to say? Maybe it was better to just imagine she'd misspoken.

Grams leaned forward over her plate, her blouse nearly touching the marinara sauce. "My Greg was a good boy."

I got where she was going. Because I didn't share her son's genes, it explained the mess I'd made. If I was *really* her granddaughter, I would never have dreamed of screwing up. I would be perfect.

"Your Greg was *her*"—my aunt pointed at me—"father. Period."

Except that wasn't entirely true, was it? I thought about the photo of Mason King on my phone. I could whip it out and show it to my grandmother right then and there. *Guess what? My real father is a famous horse trainer. A celebrity. He made a name for himself and isn't a screwup.*

Grams started to respond, but Aunt Laura held up her hands. "You know what? That's enough. End of subject. This is my house, and this gets tabled. Right now. Let's just eat our dinner and talk about the weather or the Colts or even politics."

My grandmother's lips pursed, but she leaned back in her chair and started in on her lasagna again. A small, red sauce stain blotted her blouse, and I wondered if it would ever come clean.

Chapter
12

I WAS IN BED when Tessa's text came in.

> Tessa: Are you asleep?
> Me: I'm trying but can't.
> Tessa: How did the dinner go?
> Me: Ugh.
> Tessa: That bad?
> Me: Grams said some really hurtful things.
> Tessa: I'm so sorry.
> Me: Me too.
> Tessa: You don't have to share, but you can if you want.
> Me: She thinks I'm a loser.

Almost a minute went by before Tessa responded back. I hope you know you're not. You're really smart and I admire your strength.

Me: I don't feel smart or strong.

Tessa: That doesn't mean you aren't.

I almost told her the truth of why my grandmother felt I'd let her down. Of the secret I'd carried for months now. The one Jade and Kelsey seemed to know and were holding over me. But I couldn't. Tessa believed I was smart and strong. That would all change if she knew.

Me: I don't think she knows who my bio father is.

Tessa: Did she say something?

Me: Implied I wasn't family.

Tessa: Oh, Shay, I'm sorry.

The tears came again, and I let them fall. Stanley stretched out his legs and almost pushed me off the bed, but his warm doggie body was comforting. I didn't feel quite as alone with him beside me, and Tessa's words offered solace.

I remembered how many of my classmates stood in drama class because they'd felt lonely, Tessa among them.

Me: In Drama, when Ms. Larkin mentioned lone-liness, we all stood up.

Tessa: I know.

Me: When do you feel lonely?

Another minute passed, and I stared at my screen waiting for my friend's response. *Maybe I shouldn't have asked. It might be too personal.* We were already in new territory here, and I wondered if the safety of the phone screen was allowing us to share more than we would in person.

Tessa texted, At night sometimes. The house is so quiet. Sometimes I hear my mom crying.

One time in my life I'd seen my dad really cry, and it had practically scarred me. I couldn't imagine what it would be like to listen to your mom grieve like that. I couldn't imagine having a mom period, but I tried to. It wasn't as if I could ask my friends, "Hey, what's it like?" How could you even qualify that? I knew Aunt Laura was trying, but it wasn't the same.

> That must be hard, I responded.
> Tessa: Yeah. But maybe it's normal.
> Me: LOL. I've been searching for normal ever since my dad died.

I rested my phone on my chest for a minute, and the room went black. I could hear my aunt still puttering around in the apartment. I hated that she'd had to change her entire life around just for me. She used to be able to play her favorite music at night while she worked in her own office. Now she was straightening up the corner of her living room trying not to make too much noise. *Is she counting the days until I turn eighteen and can legally move out?*

I decided to change the subject.

> Me: Hey, there's a meteor shower coming up this weekend.
> Tessa: Really?
> Me: The Leonids. Would you want to watch it with me?
> Tessa: That sounds fun!
> Me: You could come over to my house.
> Tessa: Your aunt wouldn't mind?
> Me: She'd love to officially meet you.
> Tessa: I'd love that too. I better get to bed now.
> Me: Me too.
> Tessa: Good night, friend.
> Me: 'Night.

—⚬—

"Shay!"

It wasn't Amelia calling my name.

I kept walking across the school parking lot hoping to make it to the safety of the building.

"I know you heard me, girl."

No such luck.

Jade stepped into my path next to a red pickup truck that belonged to Matthew Lucas, my World History teacher and the robotics team head coach. He went to Izzy's church.

Kelsey came up behind me. "Think she's spontaneously gone deaf?" She pushed me from behind toward Jade, hard enough that I stumbled to catch my balance, yet not so hard that it couldn't look like she'd accidentally bumped me.

"If I'm not mistaken, I think she's ignoring us. Is that right, Shay?"

"I have to get to class."

They both laughed. "Why would you ignore us?"

"Look, I don't know what you want from me." I swung around so I could have both of them in my line of sight. I couldn't back up because of the truck, and they were two feet from me, but if this became a problem, I could probably scream loud enough for someone to come running. But if I did that, I'd be the sissy, nerd girl who cried wolf, and I knew Jade and Kelsey would concoct some story that made me look bad or sound like a liar.

"Did we say we wanted something?"

I actually let out a curse word.

"Oooh," Kelsey said. "She's not such a prude."

I'd feel guilty for that later, I knew. My dad had taught me to keep my mouth clean. *What if Tessa or the other girls heard me say that?*

"Just stop," I said. "How do I know you're not playing me, that you have nothing on me at all, and this is all some stupid game?"

Kelsey suddenly grabbed me by the front of the coat and stuck her face inches from mine. She called *me* a name.

"You really want to test it?"

It took everything in me to keep from shoving her away, but I knew reacting would provoke another fiery encounter.

"Get your hand off me."

Kelsey let go with a laugh, then brushed the front of my coat like she was trying to help me out all along. Then she told me exactly what I didn't want to hear. It was clear. My secret was not a secret after all.

"Believe me now?"

I didn't move. She wasn't bluffing.

I'd been counting on her bluffing.

"I . . . don't get it," I said, hating the tremor in my voice.

Kelsey made her own voice tremble to mock me. "What don't you get now, orphan girl?"

"Why you're doing this."

Jade elbowed Kelsey. "It's too fun keeping you guessing."

They both left me there, nearly shaking with anger. Maybe that was the whole point. Not to get anything from me but just to soak in the feeling of power. Still, I did not want the whole school knowing why I'd ended up moving to Riverbend.

Tessa met me at my locker, and she was all smiles.

"I haven't watched a meteor shower in ages," she said.

I was determined not to let her see how shaken I was. I amped up my voice to match hers. "So you've seen them?"

"Oh, yeah. My dad and I . . ." She started to grimace but then seemed to catch herself. She was getting better at making his absence the new normal in her life, but I knew it still hurt. Her dream father-daughter trip to Iceland with him had fallen through because of his affair, and he'd taken his new girlfriend instead. "He and I used to drive outside the city limits to where the sky was dark. We watched the Geminids one year freezing our butts off on the roof of the car."

I laughed. "Ever seen the Perseids?"

Tessa shook her head.

"Me either! Every stinkin' year it's either rainy or cloudy."

"Will we even see them at your house?"

"Not perfectly, but I think my aunt will let us use her balcony. We might be able to see a few from there."

We agreed to meet Saturday evening. She'd have to stay the night since the best viewing was in the predawn hours. I actually wasn't sure how I felt about having a friend sleep over. We didn't know each other *that* well yet, but maybe that was the point. Friendships were tested in the wee hours. If we didn't drive each other crazy, then we could know ours would last.

I thought about inviting Amelia and Izzy to come along as well, but that felt like too much too soon.

"I looked into that stable near my house," Tessa said right as the last bell rang. I was surprised she'd stayed to talk to me through the first bell. Punctuality was important to her.

"Really?"

"It's small, but you should go see it."

"Maybe I will."

I walked into World History and took a seat in the back, like I usually did. Izzy waved at me from her seat near the middle, and I returned it. I tried to focus, but every time I looked at our teacher, Mr. Lucas, I thought about Jade and Kelsey accosting me at his truck.

I stared at Izzy's wild and curly hair, imagining her reaction if she knew my secret. Izzy was almost always bubbly and cheerful. Her Snow-White Dwarf's nickname might be Happy. If I just straight up told her the truth, I could see her being empathetic and concerned about my well-being, but likely she'd give me too much attention.

She was a good Christian girl too. *Didn't I just prove in the parking lot when I cursed that I wasn't? I'd made Jesus my Savior as a kid and decided to stick with that as I grew up, but what did it really mean now?* God hadn't kept my dad from dying, and if I was honest, I didn't know what I thought about that. But if I shared those doubts with someone like Izzy, she might quote a bunch of Scriptures she'd memorized in Sunday school about how God was trustworthy.

I believed God was real. I believed the Bible was true. But did God *really* love me? Why would He? I hadn't done anything to deserve it. And while in my heart I knew that was the whole point of Jesus' sacrifice, that it was by grace and all that, reconciling the awful things in this world wasn't easy.

At all.

Chapter

13

MY AUNT WAS WAITING AT THE CURB in her red Jeep when I walked out of school. A few snow flurries drifted from the slate-tinted sky.

"What are you doing here?" I hadn't known she was coming.

"Get in!" Aunt Laura said with a laugh.

I spotted Jade exiting the building, so I quickly jumped into the passenger seat. Stanley stuck his head forward from his position in the back seat to rest his head on my shoulder. He licked my cheek. I didn't mind one bit.

"Stanley's got a date," my aunt said.

"A . . . what?"

"Someone's interested in adopting him."

My heart sank.

Aunt Laura pulled out of the school lot onto the road. Her turn signal clicked, and she glanced over at me. "I told you not to get attached."

I reached up and pet the big greyhound's head. His ears were as soft as a rabbit's. I'd only known him for a few short days, but he'd already wriggled into my heart. Yeah, he stole half my bed at night and sometimes knocked things down with his tail, but the look he gave me when he squeaked his toy, like a little kid hoping I'll play catch, was the purest sort of joy I'd ever seen. Even Amelia's exuberance couldn't compare.

"How do you do this?" I asked.

"First time for me, too." My aunt's earrings jangled as we drove over a pothole. "The way I see it, giving him a home temporarily allows me to help even more dogs like him. These dogs sometimes come straight from the track, and they've never experienced the things a lot of dogs grow up enjoying."

"Like . . ."

"Toys, for example. I think they're fun for him because he's never had them before. At least not as an adult dog."

Stanley lay down on the blanket my aunt had placed over the seats. *He'd actually raced?* It was hard to picture this couch potato revving to 45 mph.

"No toys?"

My aunt shook her head. "Racing greyhounds aren't pets."

"Was he mistreated?"

"Not necessarily, but some are. Just like with horses."

"So, he raced?"

"Yep."

"And then they just discarded him?"

"They can only race until they're three or four. Someone cared enough about him to bring him up here. He's from Alabama."

I almost laughed, imagining him with a southern accent.

We drove through Riverbend, and I settled in, lulled by the car's rhythmic movement. Aunt Laura stopped at Starbucks for coffee, and she bought me a hot tea and ordered Stanley a puppuccino, which was just whipped cream in a cup.

I giggled like a five-year-old holding it for him. His long nose went all the way to the bottom of the cup, and he smeared whipped cream all over his schnozzle.

"What do you know about these people?" I asked as we continued on our journey.

Aunt Laura told me they were a young family with twin ten-year-olds, a boy and girl. Lived near the edge of town. Had never had a dog but wanted one for their kids. No cats.

I twisted around in my seat and stared at the greyhound, picturing him somewhere else, somewhere not with me. I'd tried really hard not to let him into my heart, but who was I kidding? I could see a stray cat on the sidewalk and in sixty seconds consider it my duty to save it. Or own it.

"I know you want to meet Mason," Aunt Laura said.

I cradled my paper cup, still full of piping-hot tea.

Aunt Laura stopped at a red light. "You can understand my dilemma?"

"I guess."

"I'm not pretending to know the man now," she said. "But Mason King broke your mother's heart. I will never forget that."

"It was years ago."

She nodded. "And that's why I don't pretend to know him. People change. But the core of who we are, our personality, usually doesn't, Shay."

"But can you understand what *I'm* feeling?"

"How much did your dad tell you about your other grandfather, your mom's dad? My dad?"

"Just that he died."

"He wasn't a good guy."

"Okay."

"It's a long story, but Mason reminded me of him."

"Have you seen all his videos?"

"Most," Aunt Laura said.

"A guy like that, who helps horses, how bad can he be?"

"That's definitely a good quality."

"I just need to know," I said. "Wouldn't you want to?"

Aunt Laura sighed. "I probably would."

"Then you have to let me."

"Shay, your grandparents are still your official guardians. I'm working on that, but they'd have to be involved."

"You didn't tell them?"

We pulled onto the road of Stanley's potential family. He stood up, as if sensing the change.

"Of course they know you have a bio father, but I don't think they have a name or a face or anything else attached to him." Aunt Laura was checking the house numbers as we drove into the development. All the houses looked alike, with only the paint colors being different. One house was still under construction with Tyvek covering its exterior, and men worked on the roof. "Honestly, I don't think they want to even consider he exists."

Maybe I was being stupid. I should let the sleeping dog lie, no pun intended. *Do I really want to mix up my life even more than it is already? My dad is gone. I should just accept it and move on. Mason King is a complete stranger to me, and yet . . .*

We pulled into the driveway of the home.

"I'll stay out here," I said.

"What, really?" Aunt Laura pulled up the emergency brake and attached Stanley's leash to his collar. "Don't you want to meet them at least?"

"No thanks."

I didn't tell her I thought I was going to cry. *That wouldn't exactly be of much help, now would it?* The front door of the house opened, and someone waved at us.

Stanley wagged his tail.

Aunt Laura didn't push me, and as she walked the lanky grey-hound inside, I couldn't keep myself from bawling. I knew my tears were for more than Stanley, but I couldn't even begin to narrow down everything that was wrong with my life.

Chapter
14

"I'M SUPPOSED TO HELP YOU TODAY." Amelia's hug squeezed me so hard that her sweater, which felt like some sort of wool, scratched my face. Two days had passed since my meltdown outside Stanley's potential adopters' house. It was Friday, and I was ready for school to be over.

"Whoa, hold up." I broke free and eyed my friend. I'd barely gotten through the door of drama class before Amelia grabbed me. "Help me with what?"

"Class, silly!"

"But—"

"Ms. Larkin noticed you were having some trouble, so I offered—"

"I'm not having trouble."

Amelia cocked her head. "You are."

I laughed out loud.

"What?"

I covered my mouth with my hand. I'd barely slept the past two nights, and my exhaustion was apparently giving me a case of the sillies.

"What's so funny?" Amelia looked down at herself. "Is it my outfit?"

"No, no." I would never laugh at someone's clothes, though Amelia's choices in fashion always did intrigue me. Things rarely matched, but somehow, she made them work. She followed a lot of fashion designers online I'd never heard of, so I didn't question her taste. *Just look at how far my fashion choices got me.* Exhibit A: Jade's Instagram feed, posted for all her friends to mock.

"I'm sorry." I tried again to keep the laughter at bay, but it was futile.

"Shaaaay!" Her voice whined, and that did it. I erupted in giggles, which was so out of character for me, but it felt so good and needed.

"You . . . looked . . ." My classmates were staring at me now. I needed to get this under control. *Breathe, girl. Don't look at your friend.*

"Felix." I barely got the name of her Labradoodle out.

Amelia was laughing now too. "What about him?"

"When you cocked your head." I did my best to calm myself, barely succeeding. "You looked . . . just like him."

Amelia stared at me with wide eyes for a second, and then we both lost it.

A full minute later I finally gasped for breath. "Wait, seriously? Ms. Larkin said I needed help?"

"She didn't really have to, but yes."

I groaned. My abs actually hurt from the laughing. "It's really that bad?"

"Shay, every time you stand in front of anyone, you look like you're about to be run over by a truck."

"Gee, thanks."

"You have to loosen up."

Tell me something I don't know, Amelia. I wasn't sure how to break it to her how hard this whole drama class experience had been for me. I barely managed the One Act, and I certainly didn't want to do another, let alone a full-on play. But Amelia dreamed of being on a stage, preferably Broadway. Sometimes it felt like we were from different planets, or countries at least. Like she was from warm and sunny Brazil, and I lived in Antarctica.

Izzy and Tessa joined us a minute later, and Amelia proceeded to tell them how much "help" I needed. The laughter from earlier faded.

"I can meet with you after school, and we can do some improv," Amelia said. "Brie and Presley say improv is the best way to deepen your talents."

Wait, who? Were those the upperclassmen she'd sat with at lunch a few weeks ago?

"I can't," I finally said.

Technically, I could, but I wanted to spend some time with Stanley. He wasn't officially being adopted yet, but things had gone well with the family, and I didn't know how much more time I had with him.

"Why not?" Amelia prodded. "It's important."

"To you maybe."

"Shay, it should be important to *you*."

A match flamed inside me. *Excuse me? What gave her the right to —*

Izzy took a step toward us. "Let's go sit down and talk more later, okay?"

"There's nothing to talk about," I snapped, and I could feel my friends looking at me like I'd just declared I wanted to go skinny-dipping or something.

"Somebody's moody," Amelia muttered under her breath.

I saw Tessa elbow her, but she was right. *How could I go from laughing uncontrollably to major PMS mode in five minutes?* It wasn't fair to Amelia, I knew. I mumbled a "Sorry" that I really did mean, but I glanced around the room and realized I hadn't spent a single minute in this place feeling like I belonged. I just got through it. *I enjoy my friends and sometimes we have a little fun, but who am I fooling? Drama is not for me. I seriously need to talk to Ms. Larkin about dropping her class. Was it too late for that? Would it affect my GPA?*

Somehow I got through class and managed to escape the school building without having to talk to anyone beyond a quick "See ya next week" or "Have a fun weekend."

By the time I walked back to the bookstore, my mood had mellowed a little, and I decided to cut through the store. Books generally made me happy, but lately I was finding it harder to read for pleasure. One of the things I missed the most about my dad was sharing books and talking about the stories as we read them. He'd been a voracious reader of all kinds of books, fiction and non-fiction, and he got a lot of free copies because of his design work.

Reading didn't hold the same joy without someone to share it with.

"Hey there, Shay."

The college-aged clerk who worked for my aunt most evenings waved at me from behind the register. Her name was Ginny, and she had tattoo sleeves up both her arms and played guitar in a rock band. But her hard exterior hid a soft inner core, and she'd babysat Stanley whenever he hung out in the store, talking to him like he was a child.

Ginny took one look at my face and grimaced. "One of those days?" she said.

I dropped my backpack on the floor and flung myself into the leather chair set up in front of the glass display window where Matilda had curled up for a nap. One other book browser, an old lady wearing a purple hat, browsed the cookbooks, but the store was oddly quiet and peaceful. I had a few minutes' reprieve before the after-school crowd showed up. Tonight, a local thriller author was doing a book reading and signing, so I imagined the place would fill up by then.

I was glad business was good for my aunt, but I wished the store was this quiet more often.

"I want to quit Drama so bad," I said, rubbing my eyes.

"Why's that?"

"How long do you have?"

Ginny grabbed a stack of hardcovers and a handful of Sharpies. She made her way over to the author table set up for the book signing. The featured book was *Whence the Night Comes* by D. L. Morrows. *Why do authors use their initials instead of their real names? If I wrote a book, I'd stick with Shay. It was unusual enough.*

"D. L.," I said. "What's it stand for?"

"Hmm . . . the big mystery." Ginny stacked the books on the table and grabbed a little stand for one copy propped up front and center. The cover featured a misty lake and a woman's silhouette running toward it. The typography was typical blocky thriller. *Not bad, though I bet Dad could've spiced it up somehow.*

"You don't know?"

"Oh, I do."

I rolled my eyes. If I had an older sister, she might tease me the same way, so I tried not to mind.

"How badly do you want to know?" Ginny kept a straight face.

"Not that bad."

She came around the table and crossed her arms, staring down at me. "Your aunt wants you to clean the bathrooms and sweep the storeroom."

I ducked down into the chair, pulling my face into my sweatshirt. I wanted to curl up in a ball and go to sleep for a year. Aunt Laura paid me to do a few hours of work each week, which was far better than an allowance, she said. It would teach me responsibility and give me a good work ethic. I honestly didn't mind most days, but my lack of sleep was catching up with me big-time. I'd probably offended my friend, who was just trying to help me today, albeit rather brusquely, but still.

"It's Dwight, by the way," Ginny said, moving behind the register to ring up the purple-hat lady's purchases. "And the L is for Lloyd, I think."

Okay, D. L. was a little more mysterious, and for a thriller writer, that was probably a positive. Maybe I'd check out the novel later. If it wasn't too scary. I'd read Frank Peretti's *The Oath* with Dad and had a nightmare about a dragon chasing me across an open field.

I pulled out my phone and decided I was feeling too lazy to type up a text. I started a video, still huddled down in the armchair.

"Sorry for being crabby today," I said. "Want to hang out tonight and do homework in our usual spot? I'll be here."

I smiled to myself. *Some teens party on Friday nights or stay up super late. Our group does schoolwork together. So exciting.*

A few minutes later I climbed up the stairs and crashed in the apartment with Stanley. Tessa said sometimes she felt lonely at night. Today was my day. I'd been surrounded by people since before eight o'clock but still felt like the one ugly duck in a flock of swans.

Maybe I'd grown up sheltered or spoiled or whatever with my dad working at home and being around more. I'd never felt alone. If he went on a business trip, I usually went with him or stayed with my grandparents.

But he wasn't here now . . . an aching fact I felt every single day.

Chapter

15

AMELIA PLOPPED DOWN onto the yellow beanbag chair in our little alcove at the bookstore, and I felt a whoosh of air hit me from the movement.

"Did you know that *The Phantom of the Opera* is the longest-running Broadway show?"

Izzy had already claimed the second beanbag chair, so Tessa and I were left with the love seat. I dragged the small end table closer so I could spread out my homework. Tessa didn't seem to mind having no table, and Amelia and Izzy hadn't even pulled out their papers yet.

"Wait, I thought it was *Chicago*," Izzy said.

I leaned toward Tessa. "Here they go."

Amelia shook her head. "That was the second-longest."

"But *Lion King* is the highest-grossing," Izzy added.

"Over 1.4 billion," Amelia said in agreement.

I thought I would mix it up a bit. I leaned forward. "But . . . here's a fun fact I bet you don't know."

All eyes turned toward me. I made them wait a few seconds. "The fastest speed ever achieved by a horse was 55 mph."

Amelia groaned. "Musicals, Shay! We're talking musicals."

Tessa elbowed me playfully. "Yeah, Shay. Get your head in the game."

I laughed, hoping to make up for my crabbiness earlier. I was still feeling my exhaustion practically in my bones, but sometimes you just had to enjoy friend time no matter how you were feeling.

I looked around at the girls who'd adopted me into their lives. We were as different from each other as our fingerprints, but somehow, we clicked. Still, I was the newest to the group and most introverted. I knew for a fact it definitely wasn't easy for people to get to know me. Amelia and Izzy were open books, and Tessa was at least half-open. But I felt like the pages of my life were sometimes glued shut, and I had to work hard to pry them apart for people.

"*The Phantom of the Opera*," I said. "Lindsey Stirling did that song—"

"Yes!" Izzy reached up and high-fived me. "Love that one."

Score for me.

Time to dampen things.

"I'm thinking about quitting Drama," I nearly whispered.

Amelia and Izzy didn't seem to hear me, but Tessa did. I glanced over at her, and her eyebrows rose. She mouthed, "Seriously?"

"What did you say?" Amelia asked.

"Um . . . we really should start homework."

"Spoilsport." Izzy unzipped her backpack and pulled out a wad of papers. We actually tried to get some work done, but my concentration was failing along with my will to stay awake. By eight o'clock I could barely keep my eyes open.

"Call it a night?" Tessa said.

"What? We're just getting started," Amelia chimed.

Izzy snapped her textbook closed. "Can we please, please meet Stanley?"

I gathered up my homework and stuffed it into the messenger bag my dad gave me for my twelfth birthday. I usually stored the bag in my backpack so I could keep my papers and textbooks separate.

Okay, that very much puts me on the spot. My brain zinged through the excuses I could give of why I couldn't bring my friends up into the apartment, but my aunt had specifically said I could have them over anytime I wanted.

"Uh . . . I guess," I finally said.

Izzy jumped up like a kid who'd been told she was going to Disney World. "Oh, my stars, I have been waiting for this for so long. He's so adorable."

I'd sent her a dozen photos yesterday when I had a mini photo shoot with the greyhound. I wanted to remember him when he was gone.

"I better check with my aunt," I said, but when I went to find her, I realized the author event was underway, and she was hovering in the background making sure everything ran smoothly. She didn't need me bothering her.

A minute later I led our ragtag group up the stairs and into my world. Stanley met us at the door, and just like I had when I first saw the dog, Izzy dropped to the floor to greet him.

I smiled. "He loves people."

Tessa didn't have any pets since her mom was allergic, but she was the type of person who could just sit in a room and animals would be drawn to her.

My friends spent a few minutes loving on Stanley, and he soaked it up. Matilda was nowhere to be found—probably downstairs rubbing up against people's legs at the event, hoping they'd drop a cookie crumb or something.

"This is so cozy," Izzy said, waving to indicate the apartment.

Was that shorthand for "small"? I knew Izzy's home was a five-bedroom, two-story house with a huge yard in the same neighborhood as Tessa's. And Amelia lived in a home that was probably at least three times the size of this apartment.

I knew I shouldn't have been, but I suddenly found myself self-conscious about our meager living situation. I'd never had a lot of money for nice things, and I was always okay with that. Dad made enough to provide everything I needed, but it's not like I got a new wardrobe every year. I'd only gotten new clothes if I grew out of the old ones.

I thought about Jade and how she'd made fun of me at school. Here I was, wearing my jeans and a sweatshirt, and my friends all had better fashion sense. Tessa rocked sporty feminine without even trying, Amelia's flamboyant colors and mismatches were so bold and *so her*, and Izzy's cute leggings and Marvel hoodie genuinely expressed her playful, creative nature. *Why would they even want to be friends with boring Shay?*

Tessa turned toward me to confront my earlier utterance. "Why do you want to quit Drama?"

Amelia's and Izzy's heads both snapped up to look at me from where they were sitting on the floor with Stanley. Tessa and I sat on the sofa.

"What?" Amelia gasped.

"You can't quit," Izzy added.

I held up my hand. "Guys, be real. I'm horrible at it."

"No, you're—"

"Amelia, you told me today I needed help."

Tessa prodded me again. "It doesn't come naturally for me either."

"But you can actually do it," I said. "Amelia's right. I can't get up in front of anyone—I'd rather I *did* actually get run over by a truck!"

I was being dramatic, I knew, but it was true. It's why I hated games like charades and Cranium.

"Sometimes you gotta push through," Izzy said.

"That makes it worse for me. If I push myself, I freeze, and then I start to think about all the ways I'm doing it wrong and overthink everything."

Amelia climbed up onto her knees. "But isn't there a part of you somewhere deep inside that finds it liberating to pretend you're someone else?"

"No."

"Really?"

"I have a hard-enough time being myself."

Izzy giggled, and I forced a smile, going along with them, letting them think I'd meant it as a joke.

Tessa sighed. "I'm not sure you can get out of the class at this point, even if you want to."

"Besides, we'd miss you!" Amelia looked up at me with sincere eyes. Then she slapped her leg with her palm. "No, I won't have it. You are not allowed to quit!"

"Okay, look. Be brutally real. Do you honestly think I have *any* talent for acting?"

My friends were quiet, and even though I'd asked for their opinions, I wasn't entirely sure I wanted them to be honest.

"I think," Tessa said, "that you haven't discovered what you're good at yet."

"But definitely not acting."

Izzy stood up too, and Stanley jumped up with her. "We're all self-conscious sometimes. That's normal."

"No, normal is feeling butterflies in your stomach." I ran my fingers through my hair. "I've got a swarm of snow geese inside me."

"Flock," Tessa said.

"What?"

"It would be a *flock* of geese."

I smacked her in the arm, and she laughed.

"I'm being serious," I said.

Amelia stood up. "So are we."

My three friends all were staring at me, and even though I knew they cared, I wasn't sure if that mattered at this point. Drama and me didn't get along.

"I only took the class because I had to," I said.

"Let me talk to Ms. Larkin," Amelia said.

I'm not sure if I like that idea either. I already feel like Amelia went behind my back a little when she was recruited to "help" me.

"At this point I don't even care if I get a good grade," I said.

"What about college?" Izzy asked. "You need a good GPA for that."

"I don't care about college either."

Tessa scooted closer to me. "Shay, it's okay to be frustrated, but don't make any rash decisions, okay?"

They didn't know how much I'd been thinking about this. It wasn't rash. It was practical. I hated drama class. Saying that, even in my mind, wasn't easy, but it was true.

I leaned back into the sofa and closed my eyes. I was so tired.

"Hey, let's call it a night," Tessa, the ever practical, said.

Izzy and Amelia both hesitated, as if they felt like they needed to stay to talk me out of my madness. In some ways I wanted them to leave, but as they got up to go, I felt the sudden urge to drag out our visit if only to cling to their kindness.

"Sorry," I muttered at the door.

"For what?" Tessa said.

"I'm just exhausted."

My friend gave me a kind smile, but I didn't have the energy to return it.

Chapter

16

I SLEPT IN ON SATURDAY MORNING. It wasn't intentional, but maybe I needed it. Aunt Laura left me a note telling me she had to leave for a women's business breakfast she attended once a month but would be back before noon.

I needed to find something to keep me occupied until Tessa came over this evening. I pulled out my phone and checked my emails. I didn't pay much attention to my inbox ordinarily, but I had subscribed to a few newsletters and tried to keep up with them.

At the top of my inbox was Mason King's weekly update. My heart jumped a little when I saw it, and I clicked it right open.

The first line stood out: *New tour stop added!*

When I saw the location, I'm pretty sure my mouth dropped open.

Cumberland County Fairgrounds, Riverbend, IN.

The date was two weeks from today.

What?!?

I scanned the rest of the email for any additional info, but there wasn't any. I was on Mason's website in a flash, where it confirmed the new tour date. *The fairgrounds were only twenty minutes from here!*

I jumped up, and Stanley lifted his head from his circular, plush bed on the floor. I started pacing the kitchen. *My aunt has to let me go. Even if I don't meet him, I could at least see him in person. If I propose the idea to her like that, maybe it would fly, and she'd consent. Would my grandparents really have to be involved? What if I got a seat close enough that he could see me? Would he know who I am? Do I look enough like my mom for him to guess? What would Dad think if he knew?*

My hands were literally shaking at the idea. I had to tell someone. I grabbed my phone and tapped out a text to my friends:

> **Guess what???**

It took less than thirty seconds for the responses to come.

> Amelia: **What?** 😊 🙏
> Izzy: Yeah, what?
> Me: **Mason King added a tour stop in Cumberland County!!!**
> Tessa: **Seriously?**
> Me: **Not joking.**
> Amelia: **Are you going?**
> Me: **I want to so bad!**
> Tessa: **Does your aunt know?**
> Me: **Not yet.**

Do I really have to tell my aunt? What if I just go? Isn't this my decision?

Amelia: This is so exciting! You're excited, right?

Am I?

Izzy: Can we go with you?

I stared at my phone, startled by Izzy's question. I hadn't thought about having my friends along. I don't know why, but I pictured myself alone, even though I knew my aunt probably wouldn't let me go by myself. *Then again, would she let four teenage girls go together?*

Me: I'm still figuring it all out.
Amelia: What's to figure out?

I wasn't sure if any of them could fully understand my predicament. Amelia's parents were busy, but they were there for her if she needed them. Same with Izzy's. Tessa's mom was definitely rattled by her husband's infidelity and their upcoming divorce, but she was surviving. And Tessa's dad was also still around. She could call him in a pinch, and even though they weren't on good terms lately, he'd still be there for her.

I didn't have any of that. Sure, my aunt was doing her best, and maybe in their own way my grandparents were too. But I had *a lot* to figure out. It annoyed me that Amelia would ask why it was a big deal to me.

Me: There's just a lot.

I almost smirked. The story of my life these days.

———※———

Aunt Laura walked in the door and dropped her keys, cell phone, and bag (she didn't like calling it a purse) on the kitchen counter. I was lying on the sofa reading *Whence the Night Comes*. I hadn't decided if it was too creepy for my taste, but I was close to saying, "Yes, it is."

I laid the book spread-eagle on my chest. My aunt grabbed a Diet Coke from the fridge, cracked it open, and came over to me. She pointed at the sofa, and I moved my legs so she had room. She'd dressed up more than normal for the breakfast, wearing black slacks, a starched, hot-pink top, and a plaid blazer to top it all off.

She dropped onto the sofa and took a long sip from her soda can. "We need to talk."

"Okay . . ." I sat up. *I don't like the sound of this.*

"I'm sure you saw his newsletter."

"Um . . . whose newsletter?"

My aunt gave me a good impression of what I imagined was a "Mom look."

"I saw it," I said.

"I'm guessing you want to meet him." Aunt Laura rested the can on the sofa's armrest. "I get that. I really do. I'd feel the same way."

"Then why won't you let me?"

"I didn't say I wouldn't."

I closed the book.

Aunt Laura sighed. I was trying to be respectful toward her. She wasn't my mom, but I knew in my heart she wanted what was best for me. I felt it more from her than I did from my grandmother.

"In three years, you'll be eighteen, and I won't be able to stop you." Her voice seemed softer, distant. "I'm not sure I'd be happy with myself if you had to handle something like that by yourself."

"I just need to know what he's like."

Aunt Laura gave me a wistful smile. "I know I'm not your parent, but I do care."

I managed a nod.

"I want you to stay safe."

"Is there something you're not telling me?"

"Nothing I can confirm."

I met my aunt's eyes. "Was he bad to my mom?"

She hesitated and then shrugged. "I never saw anything. It was more in my gut."

Great.

"He seems nice to the horses," I said.

"Which is why I'm letting you go."

It took a second for her statement to register.

"Really?"

Aunt Laura chugged her Diet Coke. "Not saying I agree it's a good idea, but this is one I think you're old enough to decide."

I wanted to hug her. I almost did, but instead I settled for the biggest smile I could muster. "Thank you."

"I hope it works out," Aunt Laura said. "I really do."

"Wait, do I have to tell Grams?"

"Up to you."

I wasn't entirely sure how my grandmother or grandfather would react anyway. *It's possible they would refuse to allow me to go, but could they really reinforce that if Aunt Laura is okay with it?* They essentially gave up their right to control my life by bringing me here. Yet I wasn't looking to make waves. I wanted to do the right thing, whatever that was.

"There's this barn near Tessa's and Izzy's neighborhood," I said, changing the subject. "I was hoping I could check it out sometime, you know, to be around horses again."

"I'm sure we could manage that."

"Could I go today?"

I don't know if it was because my aunt was in a particularly generous mood or if she relished the idea of changing the subject too, but without a word she got up, picked up her keys, and waggled them at me.

"Hurry up, kid. I've got twenty minutes."

Chapter
17

WE DIDN'T TALK MUCH IN THE JEEP, but the silence was a comfortable, understanding silence. It was the first time I felt like my aunt really got me.

After two wrong turns, we pulled up to Green Tree Farm.

"What kind of a name is that?" my aunt said with a laugh.

"Guess there are a lot of green trees?"

"There's green grass, too, but that doesn't have quite the ring, does it?"

I hadn't called ahead of time, and I wasn't even sure if the farm wanted visitors, but I jumped out of the Jeep. This is one thing I liked about Riverbend. You could be in the middle of town at the bookstore, and in ten minutes escape and actually be in nature.

I waved to my aunt.

She hung out the window. "Sure you don't want me to stay?"

I think she assumed I'd called, and I didn't correct her. Worst case scenario, I'd be ringing her up in five minutes for a return ride.

"I'm good."

I turned around and took in the place. From where I stood, I could see several horses in a pasture with white fencing near a barn that looked like it held at least ten stalls and an open stable for horses to take cover in more extreme weather. An outdoor arena with a few jumps and barrels set up was only a stone's throw away. Three cars were parked in a small lot outside the barn, confirming I might actually have to talk to someone instead of just visiting with horses like I'd hoped.

The Jeep's engine faded, and I stuck my hands in my pockets. This had seemed like a good idea, but once the security of my aunt was gone, I felt nervous. Especially when I remembered the last time I'd been at a barn.

I really should've called first.

Okay, deep breath. Go for it.

I walked toward the barn. It was so quiet out here. In town I was accustomed to the hum of traffic or people talking as an ever-present white noise. Even in the apartment the silence could be interrupted at any moment by a car horn or a shouting passerby. But here? The quiet of fall had settled in, and I could hear the wind rustling the dry leaves of the oak tree towering over the parking lot. Somewhere a wind chime faintly tinkled its song. If this were a movie, some sound engineer might've inserted a horse whinny or snort into the soundtrack, but horses were quieter than most people realized. They rarely nickered or called unless one of their buddies left the pasture. Or if it was feeding time. If dinner was coming, all bets were off.

Despite my trepidation, I could feel myself relax. At least I was relaxed until the stocky, middle-aged woman came up behind me.

"Who are *you*?"

I swung around, startled. "I . . ."

Her hair was short and graying, and she actually wore a T-shirt in the chilly air. Jeans tucked into muck boots and a pair of dirty work gloves completed the look. She reminded me of a bulldog.

"You here for the job?"

"Job?"

"I'll take that as a no."

"You're hiring?"

The woman walked past me, heading toward the barn. "Stall help. Mornings."

I don't know why, but I instantly wanted to work here. *Can I manage it before school? I'll have to get up super early, and I'm not at all sure my aunt would agree since I am already helping her in the bookstore.*

"We're a private farm," the woman said, looking me up and down. "No drop-ins unless you know someone here."

"I . . ."

Why am I suddenly without words and sounding like an idiot?

"Name?" the woman peeled off her gloves.

"Shay."

"That's a new one."

It wasn't uncommon for people to wonder about my name, and I kinda liked that it was different. Izzy had giggled when I'd first introduced myself. She'd said, "Hey, Shay," and its rhyming quality amused her.

"Did you—" the woman glanced around, "—fly here or get dropped off?"

I reached for my cell phone, ready to call my aunt before she got too far. "Sorry, I didn't know this was a private—"

The woman waved me off. "Help me drop hay, and I'll show you around."

Um . . . okay.

"I'm Janie."

I returned her very firm handshake feeling like the bones in my fingers would crunch from the pressure.

"Nice grip," she said, then let me go. "You know horses?"

"A little."

Janie waved for me to follow as she opened a side door to the barn. As we passed the horse stalls, I was disappointed to see they were all empty, though it made sense. They were probably on day turnout now that the nights were cold.

"I'll drop; you stack."

Janie walked off and left me alone in the barn, and I stood there wondering why in the world she was trusting a complete stranger.

A hole appeared in the ceiling, a trap door she'd opened from the loft. Janie's head appeared, and then she called down, "Incoming!"

A hay bale dropped from the hole and thudded at my feet in a burst of dust.

"Stack it in the empty stall!" Janie called. "The one without bedding."

I did as I was told. I didn't have gloves, so the baling twine dug into my fingers, but I decided not to hesitate and just stacked the hay as best I could in the stall they'd designated for that purpose.

Thirty bales later, I was sweating under my jacket and covered in pieces of hay. A few strands had somehow made it down my shirt and into my bra, scratching and poking at my skin.

I was trying to get it out as modestly as I could when Janie came back down. She chuckled when she saw me. "Happens to all of us," she said.

"Do you give lessons here?"

"Nope." Janie brushed off the fronts of her jeans. "Just have boarders."

My shoulders dropped.

"You wanting to ride?"

"It's been a long time," I said. "I needed to be around horses again."

"Horses are good for the soul." Janie gave me another once-over, and I wondered what she saw. *Do I look like a horse girl?* I thought of Jade and how she'd mocked my clothes. Here I fit right in.

Janie grabbed a broom and started sweeping the cement aisle still littered with hay. "I've only got one in right now, but you're welcome to visit her." She pointed toward a stall halfway down the aisle.

I walked over and peeked inside. A small, dark-gray mare stood up against the back wall napping with her back leg cocked. She looked almost small enough to be a pony. *Why was she inside and not out with her friends?*

"Abscessed hoof," Janie said, answering my question as if she'd known what I was thinking. Hoof abscesses could be incredibly painful for the animal, and sometimes the only treatment was to wait until they burst and drained.

"Hi, mare," I said.

I saw her ears point toward me, and she woke up. The top half of the divided stall door was open, so the little horse limped over to me and I was able to pet her face, surprised she let me. If she was in pain, I wouldn't have blamed her for staying in her corner and not paying me any mind.

"What's her name?" I asked.

"Ava."

I rubbed the mare's forehead, and she sighed. Her skin was dark except for right on her nose, where a white patch with pink skin underneath stood out.

Janie's sweeping became rhythmic, and I just stood there with the mare until the woman had finished. I wondered what Ava's life had been like. *How many owners had she had? Was she happy?*

An hour later I climbed into my aunt's Jeep—dirty but happy. I'd needed that more than I knew. I was about to broach the subject of working here when I saw my aunt's face. She did not look happy.

"What?" I asked.

"We have a problem," Aunt Laura said.

Chapter
18

"GINNY CALLED IN SICK." Aunt Laura zipped into her parking space behind the bookstore.

I knew where this was going. My calm, relaxed Saturday was about to turn into a crazy day working in the bookstore. But after the morning at the barn, I felt I could handle it. This was where I needed to be right now, and I decided helping my aunt today was something I could give back.

"Thank you so much," Aunt Laura said and gave me a quick, sideways hug as we walked into the storeroom.

Wow. She must really be desperate.

Then Aunt Laura looked me over and cringed. "Shower first. Quick."

I laughed and ran upstairs. It surprised me that she trusted me, a Luddite math hater, with checkouts on her iPad-like kiosk, but that's where I ended up after my shower. I rang up customers and kept the free coffee and cookie station stocked. Aunt Laura kept a donations jar on the table that helped offset the cost. Around Christmas, people got generous, and she used the extra money to buy decorations and silly Santa hats. And in the rare case that there was a lot extra, she might pocket it.

Sitting behind the counter with Matilda curled up on a chair behind me, I tried not to look as bored as I felt. I loved books, but reading them was different than selling them. One plus was that from my perch I got to people-watch the patrons without appearing weird.

Book people were an interesting lot, and Saturdays brought out all ages and types of customers. Parents dragged their kids to my aunt's storytelling sessions, where she roped in one of her employees or friends to dress up as a character in the story. So far, I'd managed to avoid that fate, but before I arrived, Amelia had once come as the Cat in the Hat and dramatically read the book to eager kiddos.

College students with their earbuds and laptops confiscated any available chair or table positioned throughout the store. Some sat on the hard floor. Church ladies bought books for their women's groups, and retirees picked up bestsellers to pass the time.

I tried to finish *Whence the Night Comes* in between customers but couldn't. I'd had a nightmare about being buried alive in a coffin and decided D. L. Morrows wasn't for me.

An hour and a half into my "shift" Jade and Kelsey and two more of their friends walked into the bookstore.

Oh, man.

They were laughing and joking, and I wondered what in the world they'd want to read. Neither of the girls struck me as the bookish type, but people could fool you, as I knew far too well.

I caught a whiff of lavender perfume as the four of them walked right past without a word. Fine by me. Their group made a beeline for the alcove where Amelia, Izzy, Tessa, and I often hung out, and I wondered if somehow Jade or Kelsey knew that was our spot. Not that it was reserved explicitly for us, but it felt like a violation to have those girls sitting in our beanbag chairs.

"Excuse me, miss?"

I hadn't even seen the guy in the tweed coat walk over. He stood right in front of my counter and held out two military biographies.

Is it weird that it unnerves me I can't see the alcove from here? I felt vulnerable not knowing where Jade or Kelsey had landed. Aunt Laura was back in her bookstore office working on inventory or something like that. I could call her if I needed anything, but I was determined to handle whatever came myself.

The customers thinned after a while, and Jade appeared.

"You're out of coffee," she said, pretending to pour a cup in the air.

I'd *just* made a fresh pot twenty minutes ago. I came around the counter and headed to the coffee station. It wasn't anything fancy, but my aunt felt it was important to provide something warm and enticing to her customers. We only had to clean up a few spills a week.

"Oh, and the cookies are gone too." Jade headed back to her friends, and I quickly poured more French roast grounds into the maker and refilled the cookie tray with chocolate chip and oatmeal raisin.

I glanced at the donation jar.

Empty.

At least a couple of George Washingtons had peered out at me through the glass when I'd last filled the coffee pot. Before I could stop it, a flame burst in my gut. I glanced toward the alcove where Jade and Kelsey and whoever the other girls were sat talking in whispers and sipping paper cups full of the coffee I'd made.

Maybe I should've thought it through a little bit more, but I dumped the coffee grounds into the filter, poured spring water into the tank, flipped the switch, and grabbed the empty donations jar. I marched over to the girls.

"Where is it?" I demanded, holding out the empty jar.

Kelsey, her awesome hair looking like a lion's mane, glanced up at me from the closest beanbag. "Girls, this is the kid I was telling you about."

Heat rose up my neck.

"Cut the bull and give it back," I said.

"I don't know what the heck you're talking about," Kelsey said. Except she didn't say *heck*.

There was something about her face. She wasn't smiling per se, but I could see the smirk in her eyes. It was like I had stepped on a bomb, and she held the detonator switch. I wanted to kick her leg, which was inches from my booted foot.

Stop it, Shay. Stop it now, while you can.

I tried to relax myself by consciously breathing.

"I'm going to ask you one more time." Deep breath in. Long breath out. "Give me back the money you took from this jar, or I will tell my aunt."

"Will you?"

"And she will not be happy."

Kelsey laughed. Her friends joined in.

"I didn't take your stupid money," Kelsey said.

"Yes, you did."

She stretched her arms above her head and yawned. "Seems more like something *you'd* do." Kelsey stared up at me. *How can I be the one who feels small when she is the one on the floor? I know for a fact she took the cash, but there is absolutely no way I can prove it.* Her word against mine. My aunt would believe me, but she'd need proof. Kelsey could've hidden it anywhere.

Walk away. That's what I should do. I know it, but it will take all my strength. It's one thing to pick on me. But screw over my aunt or my friends? No, that is not okay.

I decided to try one more time.

"My aunt needs that money. Please put it back."

Jade, who was sitting on the love seat like Amelia had the other night, gave me a mock frown. "Aw, I'm sorry. It must be hard to be poor."

"She's not poor; she just—"

"Shay." Kelsey shifted on the beanbag. "We're kind of trying to have some girl time here. No offense, but if you want to talk to me, school would be a better place."

She gave me the sweetest smile, and if I didn't know better, I'd think she might almost care.

I wanted to throw the jar at her head, but I managed to control myself and went back to the checkout counter, where two people were impatiently waiting.

"Sorry," I muttered.

I couldn't think for another ten minutes as the line grew. It was good business for my aunt, but I was so frazzled that I gave the wrong change to two people. I sat down once the line cleared. *What am I supposed to do? Tell my aunt without proof? They'd just lie, and what if I remembered things wrong? Is that possible? Kelsey's denial seemed real, but I know what I saw, right?*

My phone vibrated with an incoming text, so I checked it. Tessa.

> Still on for tonight?

I texted back: Yes, definitely.

> Tessa: Looking forward to it! Can I bring anything?
> Me: Me too, and nope. Pizza okay?
> Tessa: Sounds good. See you in a few hours.

I kept my phone out on the counter. Seeing Kelsey and Jade and their buddies made my heart yearn for the safety of my own friends. We might be labeled prudes or churchies or something even crasser by the likes of Jade or Kelsey, but I realized maybe I didn't mind. Except I am the one with the secret. *I don't want to end up as a snobby bad girl, but do I really fit in with my friends?*

I tried to distract myself with a Mason King video, but that was a mistake. I'd managed to forget about him for most of the day, and it all came crashing back into my mind when I saw him effortlessly riding a mustang in a packed arena.

Then Kelsey and Jade were standing in front of me.

"You look cute back there," Jade said, snapping another photo of me before I could protest. *Like it would've made a difference, but weren't there rules about getting someone's permission before using their likeness? Probably not in this stupid, digital age.*

"Oh, totally," Kelsey agreed.

"You just going to stand there, or did you have something to buy?" I was trying to sound tough, but I wasn't at all feeling it. Hopefully they wouldn't be able to tell.

Kelsey picked up a keychain with a small book stack carved from wood as its fob. My aunt found them on Etsy and arranged with the artist to consign them in the shop.

"These are neat," Kelsey said.

"They're twenty-five dollars," I said.

"Wow," Kelsey threw the fob to Jade, who caught it. "Expensive."

Jade smiled. "Handmade?"

"Yes," I said.

"Do you take Visa?"

I thought back to the analogy I'd first associated with these girls. Cats playing with mice. I didn't want to play this game, but I didn't see I had much choice. I needed to pretend they were any other customer and not let them bait me.

"All major credit cards," I replied.

Kelsey pulled a wallet out of her purse. She slipped out a card and started to hand it to me.

"Oh, wait, not that one." She yanked her hand away and stuffed the card back into the wallet, removing another. It looked like an American Express. Then she thought better of that one too and took out a maroon-colored Mastercard.

Kelsey handed it to me, and I went to take it. For a moment both our fingers held the plastic. I pulled it, but she didn't let go.

"Hold up," she said.

"Can you please just make up your mind."

She elbowed Jade beside her. The other two girls were quietly snickering. *Had they planned this?* I glanced around the room, but unfortunately, we were the only ones present. Light shone in the front window, cascading through the air and illuminating dust particles. Aunt Laura had opted against curtains since she wanted sidewalk shoppers to be able to look into the shop and get a feel for the ambience.

I let go of the credit card, and Kelsey held it up in front of her face and winked at me. "I'm thinking I don't need this after all."

I nearly rolled my eyes at her dramatics.

She leaned over the counter, dangling the key fob in front of me. Then without a word she tucked it into her pocket. Jade reached around her friend and took one of the remaining signed copies of *Whence the Night Comes* and tucked it under her arm. "My dad will love this," she said.

I felt myself starting to panic as I realized what they were doing. "You can't just—"

"Oh, but we can." Kelsey shrugged and nodded her friends to the door.

"No!" I rushed around the counter, ready to physically block their way. "I'll call the cops."

"Shay." Kelsey said my name in a condescending tone. "I told you we'd let you know how you could help us."

"You're *stealing!*"

"It's not stealing if someone else pays for it," Jade said.

Kelsey poked a finger at my chest. Hard. "That would be you, my friend."

Without thinking, I shoved Kelsey's shoulders. "Jerk!"

She stumbled backward into her besties. They managed to

keep her from falling, but the move flipped a switch in the girl. Her eyes narrowed, and she gave me a look that scared me.

"Stupid move," she snarled, glancing up at the security camera near the door.

And then all four of them left, leaving me standing there in an anxious fury.

Chapter
19

My HAND SHOOK as I rang up the last customer. I hadn't been able to stop my body's reaction, and it chased me to my shift's end. The moment Peter, the retired guy with the shaved head who worked some weekends for my aunt, arrived to relieve me at the kiosk, I dashed upstairs to the apartment hoping my aunt was nowhere to be found.

I couldn't face her right now. Couldn't face anyone.

Stanley met me at the door in a flurry of greyhound excitement, but I ignored even him and ran to my bedroom, though it wasn't really mine. It was my aunt's. Just like this store and everything in this apartment except my clothes.

I was frantic, and I flung open the top dresser drawer where I kept my wallet. It had to be enough. I yanked out the bills. Two twenties, a five, and three ones. I'd been saving it up to buy a new pair of boots, but I didn't think about that now.

Running back downstairs, I waited until Peter went to help a customer find a book on California wildlife, then tapped in the transaction for a copy of *Whence the Night Comes* and the key fob. My money barely covered it.

"Whatcha doing?"

I spun on my heels. Peter stood behind me. He used to be a city bus driver but injured his back and couldn't sit the long hours anymore. I didn't know how old he was, but he was probably older than my dad and younger than my grandfather. I think he shaved his head because he'd be half bald if he didn't.

"Gee whiz, kid, you're as white as a sheet."

I tried to smile. "Just ringing up a purchase I forgot."

"You okay?"

I really didn't want to lie to him, but I couldn't possibly tell him what was going on. He would tell my aunt, and that was not something I wanted to handle right now.

I decided I wouldn't answer either way. "I gotta run," I said.

That much was true. Tessa would be here soon, and somehow, I had to pull myself together.

Back up in the apartment I grabbed Stanley's leash, and after texting my aunt where I was going, I took him out for a walk. It's the only thing I could think to do. Except in my haste I forgot my jacket and was shivering within two minutes.

We passed Grounds and Rounds, the coffee shop my aunt had been considering partnering with to provide more than just a pot of coffee in the bookstore. I stepped inside to get warm, hoping Stanley would go unnoticed. We sat down at a corner table, and with my back to everyone, I lost it and cried silently into my hands.

Lord, please help me. I don't know how to handle this.

This wasn't happening. It wasn't. *How could I have done that?* It didn't matter that she'd provoked me or even touched me first. I'd let my inner fire, that rage I couldn't seem to control, take over, and now I was going to pay the price.

"What am I going to do?" I whispered to Stanley. He'd lain

down at my feet and patiently, faithfully, waited to follow me to wherever I took him. But I couldn't even depend on his stability. He'd be gone soon, and I'd be alone again.

"Shay?"

Oh, gosh, not another person recognizing me. I felt a hand on my shoulder and looked up to see a twenty-something woman with a head full of dark braids.

My blank stare must've clued her in that I had no idea who she was.

"I'm so sorry." The woman sat down in the open chair at my table that I had not invited her to use. "You might not remember me. My name's Zoe." She held her paper coffee cup with both hands, several trendy copper rings stacked on multiple fingers. "I'm a youth leader at Tessa and Izzy's church, and I came to the One Acts and saw all of you guys."

"Oh."

Shoot, now I remember her. I'd been so stressed at the time that I might not have recognized my own grandmother if she was standing in front of me.

"They speak very highly of you."

My friends talked about me? And said nice things?

I realized it was probably obvious I'd been crying, and I used my sleeve to wipe my eyes, hoping this Zoe lady wouldn't call me out on it or ask me if I was okay. *I was* not *okay.*

"Hey, can I get you something?" Zoe nodded toward the menu chalked on the wall.

"I'm fine, thank you."

"Seriously. You look cold." Zoe stood, her hoop earrings swooping at the movement. "Coffee? Tea? Hot chocolate?" She pointed at her own cup. "Soy latte?"

I made a face, and Zoe belly laughed. I finally told her Earl Grey tea, just to get her off my case. A minute later a steaming cup sat before me, and Stanley sniffed the air as Zoe sat in the chair across from me again. She pressed her finger to her lips to indicate she wasn't going to tell on us.

"You guys did a great job with your play," Zoe said.

I took a sip of the tea and nearly burned off the roof of my mouth.

I honestly didn't know what to say. I'd barely met this woman, and yet she acted like she was my friend. *Is it because she's a youth leader? Maybe that's what they are taught to do.*

"Do you go to a youth group?"

"No."

I wasn't up for giving explanations. If she judged me, she judged me. My aunt and I didn't go to church either, but it wasn't because we didn't love God. We just hadn't found our place, and in my aunt's case, she worked so hard six days a week and sometimes even had to work Sundays.

"You're welcome to come visit ours anytime you want."

How does she even know if I'm a Christian? I guess Tessa or Izzy told her.

I saw myself pushing Kelsey again. It was as clear and sharp as a movie. I could feel the anger pulsing in my hand and the look of disbelief flash across her face. She hadn't expected me to do that, and I wished more than anything I could take it back.

I snapped out of my wandering thoughts and saw Zoe staring at me with a concerned expression. She leaned forward slightly. "I'm not going to pry, but just know you can talk if you want."

"I don't even know you."

"Sometimes that makes it easier."

I tried my tea again and managed to swallow it down. It didn't have any milk like I normally added, so the bergamot tang was strong.

"Tessa's coming over tonight," I said.

"Mmm . . . sounds fun." Zoe's coffee-colored eyes somehow exuded the warmth my body was lacking.

"We're watching the meteor shower."

"Definitely not my cup of tea." Then she chuckled at her own joke, and it turned into that contagious laugh.

Only it wasn't so contagious for me. I was stalling, I knew. *What if something I say gets back to my friends? Are youth leaders held to some code of honor like a priest or a lawyer, where whatever you share stays with them? I don't want to ask.*

"I messed up," I finally said.

"Something we all do."

"Really bad." I couldn't look at her.

Zoe worked on her latte and just nodded, listening.

"I don't know what to do."

"Well, not knowing the full situation, I'd ask you if it's something you need to tell your parents."

At least I knew my friends hadn't blabbed about my situation to this lady.

"I don't have any parents. At least not anymore."

"Then your guardian."

Does Aunt Laura need to know? Probably. But I'm too scared I'd get in even more trouble. It's not like anything happened. Kelsey didn't fall or hurt herself, and she was stealing from the store! I was trying to stop her. That had to count for something, right?

"It's really complicated," I said.

Zoe was nodding again.

"I tried to make it right, but . . ." I wiped at my eyes again. I really didn't want to do this. Not now, and not with Zoe, though she did seem nice.

Reaching for my hand, Zoe gave it a squeeze. "Here's what I do know, Shay. There's nothing you could do or will ever do that God can't forgive. Tell Him. He wants to be there for you."

"He just . . ." I couldn't seem to complete my sentences anymore. I wanted to say God felt so far away right now, but Zoe was a youth leader, someone whose business it was to be close to God. I wasn't sure if she'd understand.

"Pardon me, miss?"

A male employee wearing a ball cap and black apron approached the table.

Zoe gave him a smile, though I knew he was talking to me.

"Unless that's a service dog, I'm going to have to ask you to leave." The guy seemed apologetic, but he stood there waiting for me to obey.

"Thanks," I said to Zoe, who got up with me. I could tell by the way she crinkled her forehead that she wanted to talk more, to perhaps be that wise confidant all youth leaders were supposed to be, but I couldn't handle that right now. *Why is it that when people are actually nice to me, I sometimes feel like running away?*

We left the coffee shop together, and Zoe looked at me like she was about to say something.

"I've got to go," I blurted. I spun around and walked briskly away from her. Stanley and anxiety my sole companions once more.

Chapter
20

TESSA ARRIVED RIGHT ON TIME at six o'clock. I could still feel my panic hovering within me, but I'd managed to push it to the outskirts. At least for now. I really didn't want Tessa to know how much I was struggling, and I wasn't even sure why.

"I hope you like supreme pizza," I said, once she walked in the door and deposited her duffel bag in my bedroom.

"I'm not usually a fan of grease, but I'll make an exception for pizza!" Tessa plopped into one of the kitchen chairs and watched me pull the pizza box from the freezer, tear it open, remove the pizza from its plastic, and set it in the oven.

My hands weren't shaking anymore, thankfully.

"How was your day?" Tessa asked.

Ugh. Loaded question.

"Okay," I said, resting my hands on the counter. I hung my head for a moment and then turned toward my friend. "Actually, that's not really true."

I waited for her reaction.

"I hear you," Tessa said.

Her voice was kind, and I relaxed a little, knowing I could trust her. I couldn't tell Tessa everything, but even just sharing my struggles with someone was freeing. *What would happen if I took a risk and told her more?*

I wasn't there yet, but I wished I was.

Instead, I told her about the barn and how I'd gotten to visit with a wounded horse. I shared about working in the bookstore, but I hesitated when I got to the part about Kelsey and Jade.

"Remember those girls you thought were giving me a hard time at school?"

"Yeah," Tessa said.

The kitchen was starting to smell like pizza, and I pulled baby carrots and dip from the fridge for us to munch while we waited.

"They're juniors, and they came into the bookstore today."

Tessa popped a carrot into her mouth. "I bet that was uncomfortable."

That is one way to describe it. Ugh. Why can't I bring myself to tell her what happened? Because it's impossible to share the whole story without revealing what they are holding over me. But would Tessa really be horrified if she knew what that was?

I ate some carrots and tried to imagine Tessa giving me the cold shoulder. It didn't seem like her, or Amelia and Izzy. But we were just starting to forge something more than a casual, superficial friendship, so it was all new territory to me. *Do I really want to jeopardize things with something that big?*

No.

That was the clear answer. I did not. I couldn't. It was a big enough step having Tessa spend the night.

"I've never really had many sleepovers," I finally said.

"Wait, what happened with Kelsey and Jade?"

"They were jerks."

Tessa made an understanding sound through her carrot

crunching. Stanley was sitting beside her begging, but she didn't seem to notice. She swallowed. "Like how?"

I went to check the pizza, turning my back on her and hoping she'd think I didn't hear the question.

"I wonder if Izzy's sister, Claire, knows them. She's a junior too," Tessa finally said.

"Maybe," I muttered.

"Let's ask." Tessa produced her phone and started tapping on it.

"Really? Now?"

"Why not?" She kept tapping.

Well, it would give us something to do.

Tessa turned the phone toward me before she hit Send.

Do you or Claire know anything about two juniors at school, Kelsey and Jade? I'm with Shay, and we're wondering.

I shrugged my agreement to send it.

Tessa did, and we waited, munching carrots.

"We sound like rabbits," Tessa said.

I laughed. "I call dibs on Flemish giant."

She started laughing too. "I'm a Holland lop."

"What?" I nearly choked.

"It's a breed!"

"I figured that."

"Here." Tessa pulled up a photo on her phone, and we both started making I-see-a-cute-animal sounds.

The phone dinged, her notification of incoming texts.

It was Izzy. I'll ask her. Hold on . . .

"Claire?" I mouthed.

"She can't hear you, Shay."

I went to playfully smack her on the arm but thought better of it. My physical altercation with Jade and Kelsey was still too fresh. *What if my instincts were off? What if something was wrong with me and I didn't know how to actually interact with my friends in healthy ways?*

Another text came in.

> Izzy: Claire knows of them, but they don't hang in the same crowds.

Tessa started tapping on her screen again, and this time she didn't show me before she sent it. She turned the screen toward me after the chirp of incoming dread.

> They've been bullying Shay.
> Izzy: What?!? No!

"I don't know if I'd call it bullying," I said, hovering over Tessa's shoulder as she texted.

Tessa looked up at me. "Then what do you call it?"

"They were talking, and . . ." *Come on, Shay.* Kelsey had actually grabbed the front of my coat. She'd threatened to tell the whole school something I was ashamed of, and now she was literally breaking the law and blackmailing me to pay for it. *What do I call that?*

> Izzy: They better not do that when I'm around!

Tessa typed, Me either! and turned it so I could see.

The oven timer buzzed. Good save. My emotions were so close to the surface that I might start crying at their kindness.

"My aunt will be up sometime soon," I said. "She wants to officially meet you."

"I've kinda met her in the bookstore."

I set the pizza down on the table and brought over paper plates and napkins. Aunt Laura didn't seem to own a pizza cutter, at least I couldn't find it, so I had to make do with a knife. I ended up making a mess and burning my fingers, but I got it cut and served us both two slices to begin.

I started to take a huge bite but then set mine down. "Do you pray before you eat?"

"Usually," Tessa said, "but it's okay if you don't."

"I feel like a heathen."

"I'm pretty sure God doesn't see it that way."

"Hope not."

Tessa chuckled. "It's our way of thanking Him for something good like pizza." She grinned. "Plus, He probably likes it just because then we're talking to Him, but it's not like it earns you points or anything."

"Okay, then can you pray?"

My friend hesitated for a second, then bowed her head. "Father, thank You for the delicious-smelling food and for the chance to hang out with my friend Shay. I ask You to bless this meal and help us to have fun and be an encouragement to each other. Amen."

"Amen," I echoed.

Have fun and encourage each other. I'd never thought of it that way before, but that was kinda the point of Christian friendship, wasn't it?

"I saw Zoe today," I said.

Tessa's eyes widened right as she took a bite of pizza, and it took her a second to chew it fully. "Wait, really? Youth group Zoe?"

I nodded. "At Grounds and Rounds."

"She's really nice," Tessa said.

"It was weird that she recognized me from the One Act. I didn't recognize *her*."

"I know, right? I wish I had a memory like that. She can remember Scriptures she memorized in first grade."

"Now I really feel like a heathen!"

We ate for a minute in silence, and it was strangely comfortable.

"You're welcome to come to our youth group if you ever want," Tessa said. "You don't have to go to our church."

I didn't want to admit to her that I didn't go to any church, but maybe it wouldn't hurt. "I don't really have a church," I said.

"What about your aunt?"

"Neither of us do."

Tessa wiped her mouth with her napkin. I felt like she was trying to decide what to say but didn't know how. I wouldn't exactly blame her for coming down on me. Ever since Dad died, I hadn't given God the same attention, which made me feel incredibly guilty. I'd sit down to read my Bible and get distracted. Or I'd read a Scripture and not understand it. If I was being honest, my relationship with God wasn't any stronger than the one with my grandmother. I didn't hate Him, but I didn't understand Him either. *What does that say about my status as a Christian?*

"Is that terrible?" I finally asked.

Aunt Laura walked through the apartment door right then, and Tessa didn't get a chance to answer.

"Hey, girls!" My aunt carried grocery bags. She held them up. "Dessert?"

"Yes!" I said, and Tessa laughed.

"Hope you like ice cream."

But it wasn't just ice cream. My aunt had purchased all the ingredients for the best sundae I'd ever had. Peanuts, chocolate syrup, caramel, marshmallows, sprinkles, bananas, and Oreo cookies. If she was in the running for "best aunt" award, she'd be getting it tonight.

Tessa and I were groaning in delight as we spooned up every bite.

"Ugh, I can't eat any more!" I said when I was finished.

"Me either."

We collapsed on the sofa, and Stanley jumped up and nestled between us. I threw a blanket over all three of us, and he didn't move. We'd decided to watch a movie and go to bed early so we could get up before the sun for the meteor shower. It was best viewed before dawn, and I didn't want to miss it.

Tessa brought *Pride & Prejudice*, the version with that actress who was in those pirate movies. "I can't believe you've never seen it," she said.

"Or read the book."

She smacked her head with her palm. "Heresy!"

"In my defense, I grew up with a single dad."

We both laughed, and it felt better than I imagined just being real and telling things like they were. Not that having a single dad was all that weird, but it was still a little unusual. And talking about him was getting easier.

By the end of the movie I was yawning.

"Did you like it?"

"Mmm . . ."

"Shay, come on. Seriously you didn't like it?"

"It was fine," I said.

She groaned. "My work here is not complete."

I'd insisted Tessa sleep in my bed, and I would use the air mattress my aunt kept in the closet. I think she'd bought it when one of her friends with children came to visit so the kids would have a place to sleep.

I wasn't sure which bed Stanley would choose, but as I lay in the dark on the floor with my friend sleeping nearby, I smiled when I felt the dog climb onto the air mattress and snuggle beside me. There wasn't much room, but I welcomed him.

Chapter
21

SOMEONE SHOOK MY SHOULDER. I jumped awake, heart pounding.

"It's just me," Tessa whispered. She leaned down over me from the bed and was trying to wake me, like we agreed, at four thirty in the morning. At least I think it was four thirty. My room was darker than Aunt Laura's coffee.

I threw my arm over my eyes, but Tessa prodded me again.

"Come on, we're going to miss it."

"Don't care."

"Yes, you do. Get up."

"Cold."

"Then bundle up."

Stanley stretched his legs, pushing me toward the edge of the mattress. I took a deep breath and threw off my covers. I'd slept in my thermals, so all I had to do was pull my jeans and hoodie over them. It was supposed to be in the upper thirties.

We shuffled quietly into the kitchen so we wouldn't wake Aunt

Laura, who'd generously slept on the sofa so we could head out onto her bedroom balcony. With coffee for Tessa and tea for me in hand, ten minutes later we were sitting outside wrapped in our winter coats, blankets around our legs.

"Remind me why this was a good idea," I said, still barely awake.

Tessa held her coffee mug under her nose. I could barely see her silhouette in the darkness, but there were enough city lights to illuminate her and also obscure the perfect view of the sky. We could still see the stars, but I knew it would be so much better away from the lights. I thought of Green Tree Farm. I bet the view out there was perfect. If only I knew that Janie lady better and could've gotten permission.

We both went quiet for a few minutes, letting our eyes adjust to the darkness. I knew I was going to have a sore neck by the time this was over, but I leaned back in my chair and tried to keep my eyes focused on one spot. The Leonids meteor shower wasn't the biggest or the best, but I still hoped to see a few shooting stars. If we were lucky.

"Are you mad at God?" Tessa's voice was soft.

I wanted to blurt out, "No," since that was the right answer, but I had a feeling Tessa would see through that anyway.

"Sometimes," I said.

"Me too."

"What?"

When she found out her dad was divorcing her mom and moving in with his old high school sweetheart—who was now having a baby with him—and when her best friend, Mackenzie, tried to commit suicide, I knew her faith had been shaken. Whose wouldn't? But somehow, I thought she'd processed all that. I'm not sure why. You didn't just get over things like that any more than I'd gotten over my dad dying.

"It's hard to trust," I said.

"Yeah."

I decided to share more. "I keep thinking, why didn't Dad have some sort of premonition to stay off the road that night? Or why didn't something, anything, stop it? God could've done that if He'd wanted, but He didn't."

Steam from her mug rose up around Tessa's face. "It makes you think about if He really loves you."

That was it exactly, but I hadn't had the guts to say it.

"How can you know something like that—whether He really loves you?" I asked.

I felt like a heretic to even voice the question. I'd grown up knowing Jesus. He'd been my Savior for as long as I could remember, and I think it was the same for Tessa. But maybe that's why we wondered. For faith to be real, you had to choose it for yourself. I knew that much. My dad couldn't make me believe any more than Tessa's parents could force her.

"I guess that's why it's called faith," Tessa said. "But it's still not easy. I mean, my dad was supposed to be an example of what a father's love should be. Is it okay to say I don't ever want to be like him?"

I nodded, hoping she knew I got it as best I could. My dad had been my hero, but I knew he wasn't perfect. And when someone dies, you tend to remember more of the good than the bad.

"It's definitely okay," I said.

Tessa went quiet, and I hoped I was doing a decent job as a reassuring friend. This vulnerability thing was new territory for both of us.

"My aunt says I can go see Mason," I said.

"No way!"

"I'm driving myself crazy imagining it."

"Well no kidding, Shay."

"I saw one!" My hand shot into the air, pointing at the faint meteor.

Tessa missed it.

We both kept our eyes on the sky, and I held my mug of tea close. The cold air made my nose and ears cold, but I was warm everywhere else. I heard a bump on the glass and saw Stanley waiting for us. I'd thought about bringing him out, but it was too cold for his thin coat of fur to keep him warm.

"The last meteor shower I watched was with my dad," Tessa said. I heard so much more behind her words than she let on. The longing for the past but also for the future that never would be. I could relate to that.

I could also tell she needed to share this stuff, and I was more than willing to listen.

"He's the one who got me into it," she added. "He loved science."

I noticed she said *loved* not *loves* and wondered if it was because his interests had changed or his relationship to her had.

"Do you see him much these days?"

"Some," Tessa said. "When I have to."

"Parents can be really difficult sometimes."

"Tell me about it."

"I guess we can be too."

Tessa chuckled.

The next meteor she caught, and I missed.

"Did I tell you I wanted to work for NASA?" she asked.

I shifted to a more comfortable position in my chair and set my now-empty mug on the decking beside me. A siren screamed in the distance. The city was waking up.

"Past tense?" I said. I still couldn't see Tessa's face very well, so I was having trouble reading her. Maybe that's what was making it easier for us to share things with each other.

"Ever since my dad left . . . it's hard to dream about anything."

"I hear that," I said.

"I mean, don't take this wrong, but in some ways, it would've been easier if my dad died." Tessa scooted down in her chair so she could stare up at the sky better. "Then there would be finality. Closure. But seeing him start a completely new life—and a new family—without us . . . without *me*. It's hard."

"Doesn't he want to see you?"

"He says so, but it's not the same."

Her family situation was hard for me to picture in some ways. I'd only ever had Dad, and even though I thought I got it, I could only guess what a two-parent life was like through my friends. But that didn't mean I couldn't still care.

"I'm sorry. We didn't come out here to talk about my family troubles." Tessa tried to laugh, but I could tell her heart wasn't in it.

"Hey." I reached out and touched her arm, this time without hesitation. "That's what friends are for."

Chapter

22

Tessa's mom picked her up for church at eight thirty.

"Want to come with us?"

Her question came completely out of the blue, and I started to stammer a response. "Um . . ." I was standing in the living room getting ready to usher my friend out the door. I glanced over at my aunt, who was sitting on the sofa with her coffee and iPad.

"Fine by me," Aunt Laura said without looking up.

I wasn't sure if it was fine by *me*. We'd just had the conversation about church attendance last night, and for a second I felt as though Tessa might be looking to change me.

"No pressure at all," Tessa added, hooking her duffel bag onto her shoulder. Her mom had texted that she was waiting in the parking lot.

I looked down at my clothes. I still wore my thermals under my jeans.

"I'd have to change," I said.

"You're fine," Tessa said, even though she herself was wearing a dark-green Old Navy dress I could never think of pulling off well.

Uh-uh. Even I wouldn't go to church looking like this. But do I really even want to go?

Honestly? Not really.

I did want to be with my friend, though. So I ran back into my bedroom and quickly peeled off my thermals and threw on a fresh pair of dark jeans. I had a nicer gray sweater with a cool zipper I pulled over a T-shirt, and my black canvas sneakers would be better than boots. The warmest coat I had was still my Carhartt, but I had no idea if that was completely taboo in Tessa's church so decided to go without.

We waved to Aunt Laura five minutes later, and I followed Tessa out to her mom's car.

"Will she mind?" I asked.

"Of course not."

Tessa knocked on her mom's window, and the woman jumped before rolling it down.

"Sorry," Tessa said. "Shay's going to come with us, if that's okay?"

I watched Mrs. Hart's face, and her eyebrows went up for a split second, but then she just smiled.

Tessa tried the door. "Mom? The locks?"

"Oh, sorry!" Mrs. Hart said, and the doors clicked unlocked.

Rolling her eyes with a laugh, Tessa went for the passenger seat. I climbed into the back, grateful I didn't have to ride shotgun.

"Are you sure it's okay?" I asked.

Tessa made an exasperated sound. "Of course!"

I'd actually been asking her mom, but Mrs. Hart didn't seem to mind. She tapped at two coffees sitting in the cup holders.

"I would've gotten you one if I'd known," she said.

Tessa pulled out hers and handed it back to me. "You can have some of mine."

"What is it?"

"Latte," Tessa said.

"Uh . . ."

"Just try it."

"Coffee is gross!"

"Oh my gosh, are you sure you're my friend? One sip, Shay." Mrs. Hart chuckled.

"I feel like you're offering me a gateway drug," I said, taking the cup. I lifted the lid and breathed in the scent. Smelled good, but taste was a completely different story.

"It's caramel," Mrs. Hart said.

I took a sip.

We pulled out of the parking lot, and Tessa twisted around to check on me. "Well?"

I didn't want to admit it wasn't all that bad. The caramel masked pretty much all of the coffee taste.

"This is like a warm milkshake," I said.

Tessa laughed again. "I might not have succeeded in turning her into a Jane Austen fan, but I can now die in peace. Shay actually tried coffee."

"This is hardly coffee!"

"Exactly," Mrs. Hart said.

I handed Tessa back her latte and sank down into the seat. I was starting to feel the four-thirty wake-up call.

When we pulled into the Faith Community Church parking lot, my adrenaline woke me up. It had been a long time since I'd been to church, and I was worried all eyes would be on me. My concerns weren't necessary. I was greeted like I was Tessa's long-lost sister, and when Izzy saw me from across the foyer, she came running over.

"Oh, my stars, Shay! What's up? I didn't know you were coming!"

"I didn't either," I said, as my friend pulled me into a hug. I honestly could get used to this friend affection.

Izzy wore a navy-blue knit dress with leggings and her favorite brown, lace-up boots. Both of my friends were dressed way nicer than me, but I tried not to worry about it.

Izzy pulled Tessa and me aside. "Are they really bullying you?"

The two of them eyed me with concern. I appreciated their care and yet wanted them to abandon the issue at the same time. The last thing I wanted was for my friends to get sucked into Kelsey and Jade's vortex of nastiness, and I certainly didn't want them to discover the dirt those girls had on me.

"I'm handling it," I said. "You don't have to worry."

"Of course we do," Izzy said.

Tessa agreed. "If you're being bullied, you need to talk to the guidance counselor or one of our teachers. They'll know what to do."

I shook my head. They didn't quite get it. "Guys, relax. It's not a big deal."

Yet I knew it was. It really was. Those girls had stolen from my aunt, and they could be prosecuted. But what had I done? Covered it up like a coward. By ringing up that purchase and paying for it myself, I was saying everything was fine. I'd given Kelsey and Jade what they wanted.

"You've watched too many movies," I said, trying to joke, but my friends weren't convinced. Tessa actually had her hand on her hip.

Music started playing in the sanctuary, saving me from having to give more lame excuses. We walked inside and found a seat together. I sat at the end of the row.

Even though it wasn't quite the same, worship for me could sometimes feel as nerve-wracking as getting up on a stage. I knew

I was supposed to relax and just focus on me and God and singing and thanking Him for everything He'd done for me, but even when I closed my eyes, I always felt like people were staring at me.

It wasn't that I didn't enjoy worship music either. Sometimes when I was alone, I pulled up a calming, worshipful song on my phone, and it grounded me. I liked my rock music too, but I listened to different songs depending on my mood.

Breathe. In and out.

I could hear Tessa and Izzy belting their hearts out beside me, and I peeked over at them. Izzy had both of her hands raised to the ceiling, and even Tessa quietly rocked back and forth, her eyes closed. Me? My spine felt like a fence post.

Oh, come on, Shay. Everyone welcomed you. You're among friends. Relax.

By the time the pastor climbed up onto the stage, I'd managed to at least breathe normally. He preached a sermon on the Beatitudes, and I tried to focus on his words. I listened closely when he said, "Blessed are those who mourn, for they shall be comforted."

I was surprised when Tessa reached over and rested her arm on me for a second. She squeezed my shoulder.

I needed to just enjoy this moment with my friends. But I couldn't seem to shake the feeling of wondering when the other shoe would drop.

Chapter
23

I DREADED SCHOOL ON MONDAY. Anxiety threaded through me on the walk over and didn't let me go as I headed inside. I just needed to keep my head down and blend in and hope Kelsey and Jade didn't find me.

I barely made it to World History on time. Izzy tried to talk to me as I walked by her desk, but she got hushed by Mr. Lucas. For second-hour Chemistry it was the same thing. Tessa caught my eye as I walked in, and I smiled at her but found a seat on the opposite side of the room.

I wasn't purposely trying to be distant, but I was exhausted. If I got through the day without crying, I'd consider it a success. None of my friends knew I planned to talk to Ms. Larkin today, and I didn't intend to tell them. They'd just try to talk me out of it again.

I made it to her classroom as early as I could, but it wasn't Ms. Larkin I found there. Wilson, a guy who sometimes helped out with stage tech, was fiddling around with the sound equipment.

"Oh, hey." He looked up when I walked in, running his hands through his shaggy brown hair.

I'd only officially met him once, but I saw him around the school. He wore glasses, and they actually looked good on him.

"Is Ms. Larkin around?" I asked.

"Haven't seen her."

I dropped into a chair. I'd psyched myself up all morning to face her. I couldn't do this anymore. Because I was mentally preparing to lay things straight with her, I'd barely been able to concentrate in any of my classes.

Wilson looked as agitated as I felt. He tapped one of the mics, and then shook his head.

"Problem?" I asked.

"I'll figure it out."

"Need any help?"

Wilson eyed me as if to gauge my seriousness. "You're Shay, right?"

"That's me. Drama-class queen."

He cracked a smile, then caught himself.

"No, you *should* laugh. I am the worst student here, and everyone knows it."

"Why do you think I do tech?" He tapped at the mic again and then handed it to me. "Can you run up on the stage and talk into this?"

I figured I could manage that with no one else around. Climbing the steps, I stood in the middle of the stage and cleared my throat.

"Talk?" Wilson prodded me.

"Um, right. Hello? Anyone out there?"

"That's good."

"Should I keep going?"

"Just a little more."

"Never buy flowers from a monk," I said, and my voice came through the speakers along with a load of static.

Wilson looked up, his hair falling into his eyes.

I tried to keep a straight face. "Only *you* can prevent florist friars."

He chuckled and shook his head—a common reaction to my occasional bad jokes.

So did Izzy and Amelia and Tessa who'd apparently walked in without me realizing. I got off the stage and handed the mic over to Wilson.

"Have you thought about doing some of the backstage stuff—instead of onstage?" he asked.

"Backstage?"

"Set design, lights, that sort of thing."

"Is that even possible?"

Amelia hooked her arm in mine and guided me over to the other girls. For some reason it annoyed me, and I pulled away from her. I really wanted to hear his answer.

"Was Shay just flirting?" Amelia said in a conspiratorial tone.

I scrunched up my nose. "What?"

Izzy giggled.

"I was *not* flirting."

"He is kinda cute," Amelia said.

I crossed my arms. "Stop."

Amelia mirrored me; her voice still low. "Do you even know what flirting is?"

"I was just talking to him."

"Since when do you—?"

Izzy rested her hand on Amelia's arm. "Hey, ease up."

I loved my friends, but I was not in the mood for teasing. I wished they could see that. And I didn't care what they said. I was not flirting. Wilson was a nice guy, and it annoyed me that talking to him like a normal human being would be considered anything but that.

More students filed in, and then Ms. Larkin gathered us all together. When I saw her, my resolve to quit the class wavered. *I don't want her to mistake me and think she is doing a bad job, but can't she see I'm not cut out for this?*

With a clap of her hands, our class started.

"Okay, everyone! Today is going to be fun!" Ms. Larkin's exuberance oozed out of her. "As you can see, Wilson is here, and that means we're using the stage and mics. First, we're going to do a little improv feeling exercise. We won't need the mics for that, though."

She produced a small green bucket, like what a kid would bring to the beach, and shook it a little. "In this bucket I have slips of paper with different feeling words. Each of you will pull a slip from said bucket and represent it in dramatic fashion up onstage. The rest of us will guess what your word is by your actions. The first person to guess correctly goes next."

If I never guessed, would I have to play along?

"And yes, every one of you will be playing even if you don't make a correct guess." She glanced at me with a grin. "We'll play until we run out of words. Who wants to go first?"

Amelia's hand shot in the air, and she waved it back and forth. No surprise there. She climbed up to the stage. It would be an interesting experience watching everyone else. Maybe I could focus on that.

My friend immediately sat down on the stage and crossed her legs. She rested her elbows on her knees, chin in her hands. Then she rolled her eyes.

"Apathy!"

"Sad!"

Amelia shook her head and started twirling her hair with her fingers. She yawned.

"Bored!" Izzy called.

Amelia jumped up and pointed at our mutual friend. "Bingo!"

"Very good, Amelia," Ms. Larkin said, clapping.

We all joined in the applause.

"Notice how she made use of her body language and facial expressions."

Izzy picked out a slip of paper, studied it for a second, then stuffed it into the pocket of her *Doctor Who* TARDIS sweatshirt. She took to the stage, and I tried not to envy her confident presence up there.

She almost danced to the center of the stage and rested the back of her hand to her forehead. Looking off into the distance, she then held both hands to her heart.

"Excited," Amelia called.

"Happy!"

Izzy started batting her eyes and dancing around the stage, still holding her heart. She looked like the heroine of a rom-com if you asked me, but I wasn't about to start guessing emotions out loud.

"Romantic?" one of the guys said.

Izzy fell to her knees.

"Lovestruck?"

"Yes!" Izzy jumped up.

On Tessa's turn she got up and dropped to her knees too. Face in her hands, she began sobbing what sounded like very real sobs.

Without thinking, I said, "Sad."

Tessa stood up and grinned down at me.

"Wait, was that the word?"

Ms. Larkin handed me the bucket, and I wanted to act out the feeling *annoyed* or *nervous*. I finally just stuck my hand in and pulled out one of the three remaining slips. I unfolded it.

Angry.

I didn't move toward the stage.

Of all the feelings . . .

"Do I have to do this?"

Ms. Larkin smiled. "Yes, Shay. But I know you can."

"Can I pick a different one?"

"The fact that you're finding it difficult means you should do it," Ms. Larkin said.

She was just being a good teacher and trying to push me to do my best, but she had no idea. None. *I can't do this. Not right now. Probably not ever.*

"Shay, you need to get up there," Ms. Larkin said in a tone that indicated she wasn't having any more of my excuses. Couldn't say I blamed her. I always balked at these exercises.

I clenched my jaw and walked toward the steps. Push through. I had to obey her and "get up there" and just do it. No thinking. My friends had done it and survived. So had just about everyone else. *Good things aren't always easy, right?*

Climbing the two steps, I hated how quiet the room had turned. My hesitation was giving me even more spotlight, if that was possible. The bored kid who'd maybe not been paying attention surely was now. Tessa, Izzy, and Amelia probably had a clue how stressed I was, but even they couldn't help me.

Angry.

I hated that no matter how desperately I tried to be a calm, easygoing girl, I couldn't keep anger at bay. When I stuffed it down, it popped back up like a prairie dog. *Why can't I just be thankful I'm alive? My life was good. I was happy. I've seen a bright future for myself. All of that was snuffed out by one careless, stupid, disgusting, pigheaded truck driver.*

I walked onto the stage.

How could he have done that? Was "just one more beer" so important? Was his life so bad that he needed to stop that night and drink away his troubles? Did he even think about anyone but himself?

I faced my peers, my teacher. And memories rose, an insistent film inside my mind, blocking what I had been asked to do.

Dad's pickup had been cool, the air conditioning welcome in the eighty-plus-degree heat outside. I'd felt excited knowing my dad and I would have time to just relax together, eat overpriced hot dogs, and watch some amazing horses. I didn't think it would be the last time I saw him. I never dreamed the last words he'd speak to me would be "Are you hungry?"

My hands balled up, and my heart pounded in my chest.

I never saw the truck coming, and Dad certainly didn't. I remember the sound most. A terrible, crunching, reverberating thud of metal against metal, metal against flesh. And then pain.

The students almost pulled me to the surface and out of the memory as they called out feelings thinking I was trying to act.

"Scared!"

"Shocked!"

I just stood there, unwilling to move. I'll never forget the last image I have of my father. Slumped forward. Propped up by the airbag and steering wheel. His eyes open. Staring at me. A trickle of bright-red blood dripped down his cheek and onto his starched, western shirt with the mother-of-pearl buttons.

They told me I passed out, lost a lot of blood from the cut on my head. Next thing I remembered was masked doctors and nurses asking me a million questions, but all I could do was ask one of my own, over and over:

"Is Dad okay?"

The weeks and months in between flashed across my mind in a whirl of emotions and feelings. Kelsey's and Jade's faces hovered in my thoughts too, and I could almost feel Kelsey's finger poking my chest again.

"Fear!"

"Anxiety!"

I heard the students guessing, but I blocked out the actual words as the fire in my belly grew into a furnace. I swung around, desperate to quench it. A few props were kept in the shadows, and without thinking, I ran over and grabbed the first thing I saw. A chair. Rickety and scarred.

Something took over me, and I grabbed that chair and ran it back to the center of the stage. I held it over my head for a second before I slammed it down onto the stage with every bit of strength I had.

The wood cracked and broke. One of its legs flew off the stage in a burst of splinters and skittered toward Amelia and Izzy, who were sitting closest. Both of them flinched. Someone gasped.

No one moved.

My chest heaving in and out, the fire instantly shut down, and overwhelming shame took its place. My eyes filled with unbidden tears, and before anyone could guess another feeling word, I ran down the steps and out the classroom door.

Chapter
24

I ran until I was outside the front of the school, panting for air and shivering from more than just the cold wind whooshing around me. I almost kept running to I didn't care where, but what little sense I had left hit me like the truck that killed my father.

I sank to the curb and held my head in my hands. If I actually ran off the property, I'd get into even more serious trouble, and the school resource officer, Deputy Packard, would probably have to come get me. I couldn't afford that. The repercussions of breaking a chair were going to be bad enough.

I tried to breathe slower, but the oxygen didn't seem to be getting to my bloodstream.

The doors of Northside High School opened behind me, and someone's shoes hit the sidewalk.

"Shay!"

It was Tessa.

"Are you okay? What's wrong?"

She sat down beside me, and I felt myself sidle away from her. "Please leave me alone."

"I can't do that."

"Please." My voice cracked. "Don't touch me."

But Tessa didn't listen. She wrapped her arm around my shoulders. I tried to pull away again, but she held on. It was like I'd been in the accident all over again, which I didn't understand. I hadn't blocked the memories. I remembered it all perfectly. *Why did that simple white slip of paper send me down that terrifying road?*

My shoulders shook, and I squeezed my eyes shut.

"It's okay," Tessa whispered.

Was it? I'd just trashed a chair and run out of class. Everyone would be talking about me.

The November air tightened its chilly fingers around us. I tried to concentrate on my breathing again and took in a deeper gulp. I managed to relax my ribcage a little bit more.

Tessa didn't let me go. She didn't try to talk to me either, which I appreciated more than she could know. She just sat there and let me breathe.

I unclenched my fingers and realized I still held Ms. Larkin's piece of paper. It was crumpled now, and even slightly damp from the sweat of my palms. With shaky hands, I unfolded it and handed it to Tessa.

Angry.

She took it from me and read the word. Then she folded her own fingers around it and silently stayed with me on the cement curb. Soon I could feel her shivering, and I knew we had to go back inside. I didn't know if I'd get in trouble or not. But class would be ending soon, and it would probably be better if I at least showed my face.

"What am I going to tell Ms. Larkin?"

We stood up, and Tessa finally relaxed her grip on my shoulder.

"The truth," Tessa said.

My whole body felt weak, like I'd run all the way to my aunt's apartment without taking a break.

"I'm really sorry," I said.

She waved me off. "Chad guessed your word, by the way."

"I bet he did."

"And it was an old chair," Tessa added.

"I hope Ms. Larkin doesn't . . ."

"She's a Christian, you know. You could talk to her."

I wasn't sure if that helped things or not, but at least she had an understanding of the concept of grace. I had a feeling I was going to need a lot of it after my outburst.

Luckily Tessa had had enough sense to prop open the heavy door with her jacket, otherwise we both would've been locked out. A minute later we walked back into the classroom, and I tried to surreptitiously sit down in the back. Tessa came with me, and it did make me feel better to have her nearby. Izzy and Amelia were looking at both of us with wide eyed concern, but it wasn't until Ms. Larkin dismissed the class that they were able to rush over to us.

"Oh my gosh, that was awesome!" Amelia grabbed me by the shoulders and gave me a little shake.

It was supposed to encourage me. I think.

"How did you do that?" Amelia seemed genuinely oblivious to my distress.

I swallowed. "Do what?"

"Shay." Her eyes widened. "You literally broke. A. Chair!"

I glanced at Tessa. "It was old?"

"I wouldn't have thought to use a prop like that. Don't tell me you can't act," Amelia said. "I knew you had it in you."

But I wasn't acting, Amelia.

"Was your word *angry*?" Izzy asked.

Tessa showed them the paper. They went on and on about my acting skills, nonexistent before, but now for some reason I have potential because I broke a chair? I was having trouble focusing and found myself tuning them out.

Everyone finally agreed to meet up at lunch, and I was left alone in the classroom with Ms. Larkin. I tried to escape before she could talk to me, but no luck.

"I will say," Ms. Larkin said with a smile, "I didn't expect that."

I think she was trying to lighten the moment, but I knew what was coming.

"What happened?"

"I . . . guess I got a little too into it."

Ms. Larkin wasn't buying it. "You looked scared. There was a lot more going on, wasn't there?"

I decided to go the Tessa route and be honest. "I really don't want to talk about it."

"I understand." Ms. Larkin gestured for me to sit down in one of the chairs, and she slid another one close and sat down herself.

I reluctantly sank into the seat.

"You can't be running out of class like that."

"I know."

"I can make an exception for you this one time, but . . ." Ms. Larkin rested her elbows on her knees and tried to look me in the eyes. "Your heart isn't in this. Is there anything I can help you with to change that?"

I hesitated. *How about let me drop the class?* But all my nerve to talk to her about quitting had splintered just like the chair. Maybe later I could muster it up again, but right now I just wanted to escape the classroom and Ms. Larkin's kindness.

"It's not your fault," I finally said.

"I don't want to see you fail, Shay, but I'll be honest with you. I need to see a little more effort. You do not have to love drama, but it's my job to help you give it a chance to impact your life."

Ms. Larkin paused for a second, and it unnerved me how she seemed to be looking directly into me. *Does that mean she actually can fail me? What will that do to my GPA? I honestly don't really care at this point, but I know I should. I should care about a lot of things, actually, but what is the point?*

My teacher let the silence spread between us. She was probably waiting for me to explain what I'd been feeling, what I'd been thinking. But what overcame me up on that stage had crawled back into a hole inside of me. The fire had been quenched.

For now.

Chapter
25

I GOT HOME FROM SCHOOL, and all I wanted to do was crash on my bed. But when I walked into the apartment, Aunt Laura met me, and the look on her face told me that wasn't happening.

"What's wrong?" I asked.

"I'm so sorry," my aunt said.

That was enough to scare me. My aunt held up her hand before I could panic too badly.

"Everything's okay, don't worry," Aunt Laura said, "but I just really wanted you to be able to say goodbye."

I frantically scanned the room and instantly knew.

"Stanley," I said.

"I had to take him to his new home."

As if my day hadn't been enough. I instantly fought back tears, wanting to be mad at Aunt Laura but unable to muster the feeling. She was just trying to help the greyhound, and I'd known this day would come. That didn't make me feel much better, though.

"They . . . are you sure they'll be good to him?"

She came over to me, and I was surprised to see a mist in her eyes too. "I think so."

"He was a good dog."

"Is," Aunt Laura said. "Is, Shay. He's going to make his new family very happy."

I knew if I stayed and talked to her much longer, I'd lose it completely, so I excused myself to my bedroom and closed the door. In that privacy I lay facedown on my bed and cried into my pillow.

Not long after, my phone buzzed in my pocket. The interruption helped pull me out of my funk, and I flipped onto my back. It was a text from Tessa.

> How are you doing? she asked.
> Me: I've been better.
> Tessa: Just know I'm here for you if you need anything.

I paused. *Why is she being so nice to me? She has her own stuff to deal with.* But I thought about how she sat with me on the curb today. Who would've done that if she didn't really care?

> Me: Thank you.
> Tessa: I wish I could help you more.
> Me: Stanley left today. ☹
> Tessa: Oh, no.
> Me: It's a good thing, but it's not.
> Tessa: I know you loved him a lot.
> Me: It feels like nothing is going right.

I stared at my phone's screen. I hadn't even begun to understand what triggered me to freak out so badly today in drama class, but at least I hadn't been alone. Tessa and my other friends had stood by me. I wondered if God had known I couldn't handle that by myself.

I tapped out another text: I'm sorry I freaked out today.

Tessa: You have nothing to apologize for!

Is that really true? I felt like I did.

Tessa: I'm glad I got to meet Stanley.

That made me cry again. He wouldn't be sleeping on my bed tonight. I wouldn't wake up and feel his comforting doggie body against mine. There'd be no more squeaky-toy fetch sessions, no more leaning on my leg until I almost fell over.

Another text came in from Tessa. Hey, do you want to go to youth group with me and Izzy on Wednesday? I can pick you up.

A tiny zip of panic hit me at the prospect of attending her church again. I'd liked the service well enough, but I hadn't felt like I fit in. *Would youth group be any different?* I remembered Zoe and her down-to-earth personality. If all the leaders had her same qualities, maybe it wouldn't be too bad.

Sure, I texted.

We signed off, her to head out to her swim meet, me to wallow in my bedroom. I ended up watching Mason King videos, trying not to spaz out over my chance to see him next week.

—◊◊◊—

As planned, Tessa and Izzy picked me up Wednesday night. Izzy's sister, Claire, drove us, and somehow we all managed to squeeze into her truck—me and Tessa in the cramped back cab, Izzy and Claire in the front. I'd met Claire a few times, and she was always cool and left us mostly alone.

"If I ever start a band, I'm going to name us Probity," Izzy said.

I fastened my seatbelt. I'd decided to just wear my favorite clothes: jeans, hoodie, cowboy boots, and my warm Carhartt jacket. It made me feel more confident, and I decided that was important tonight.

"Uh . . . that's an interesting name," I said.

Tessa laughed. "Do you want to tell us what it means?"

"Of course!" Izzy said as she whipped out her phone. "*Probity* means adherence to the highest principles and ideals."

"Oh, wow," I said.

"Basically . . . integrity," Izzy added.

"Wait a minute. Band? Do you play an instrument?"

"Yes, she does," Claire said, pulling out onto the street. "Guitar. Pretty well, in fact."

"I've been trying to get her to join the worship team," Tessa said.

"Why don't you?" I asked.

Izzy rested her phone in her lap. "I love to listen to music. If I'm playing it, I can't enjoy it as much."

"You could do both."

She shrugged.

Izzy twisted around in her seat. Her face was in the shadows. "I'm really sorry about Stanley."

"Thanks."

"Will your aunt get another one?"

I wasn't positive I could go through this again, but I hadn't asked her. "Not sure," I finally said. "I hope not."

Izzy seemed to get it. I felt bad she'd only gotten to meet Stanley once. She loved animals, but with her brother's allergies, she didn't get to be around them nearly as much as she liked. That would be practically torture for me. I couldn't imagine not being able to pet a dog or ride a horse.

"Shay, what happened today?"

There was nothing wrong with Izzy's question, but it still made me uncomfortable.

"She might not want to talk about it," Tessa said softly.

"Amelia thinks you rocked it."

Tessa was right. I really *didn't* want to talk about it.

"We're almost there anyway," Tessa added.

Izzy seemed to take the hint. "I baked some yummy snicker-doodles today after school."

"Speaking of names," I said. "Snickerdoodle. What's up with that?"

Izzy gave a little bounce in her seat. "*Joy of Cooking* says it's probably based on the German word *Schneckennudeln*, which means 'snail dumpling.'"

"Ew, what?"

"They kinda look like snails."

"They do not."

By the time Claire pulled up to the church, we were all laughing, and I welcomed it. It was great to have friends you could be honest and real with, but sometimes you just needed to laugh, too.

We parted with Claire, checked in our phones, and found seats together. Tessa and Izzy introduced me to a few other girls, and even though I tried to brand their names on my mind, I knew I'd probably forget. It's not like I was planning on attending regularly, so I wasn't even sure I'd have the chance to meet them again, but I wanted to think I could.

Zoe found us right before the Bible study was supposed to start.

"Hi, girls!" She gave me an extra-wide smile and looked like she was going to hug me, but I wasn't ready for that and reached out my hand. Zoe shook it firmly. "So glad to see you here, Shay."

I wondered what she'd thought of me in the coffee shop. *Did I seem as desperate as I felt? Would she single me out sometime during the study?*

It turns out the group had just finished a study in the book of Ephesians, and next week they were starting something else, so this week Zoe wanted to keep things casual. She read 1 Corinthians 13, what some people called the love chapter, and I inwardly winced a little bit thinking she'd be talking about dating relationships, something I wasn't interested in right now.

"When you think of true love, what do you think about?" Zoe asked.

A few of the girls giggled and gave each other conspiratorial looks. I guessed they were imagining their current crushes.

"I think about my parents," one girl chimed in.

Zoe nodded, her large, gold hoop earrings swinging. "That's wonderful."

Someone else said she thought about the characters in a recent movie she'd seen where the guy and girl fall in love and live happily ever after.

Crossing her legs, Zoe held her worn, turquoise Bible in her lap. I thought about mine slipped into the drawer of my dresser. *When was the last time I pulled it out?* I knew God didn't care if I held an actual paper Bible or read a Scripture off my phone, but I remembered a time when I kept my Bible on my nightstand. I knew reading it didn't earn me God's approval or anything like that, but a bit of guilt ate at me over my lack of attention to my spiritual growth.

"Here's the thing," Zoe said, gathering her braids and pulling them over her shoulder. "We've let the world define our view of love. I mean, let's be real, girls. Society has hypersexualized just about everything."

My friends nodded in agreement.

"The world has reduced love to romantic love." Zoe closed her Bible on her finger. "And they've reduced romantic love to sex."

Okay . . . I don't know about the rest of the girls, but these sort of talks make me uncomfortable. Had I picked the wrong night to attend?

Zoe seemed to wait for us to digest her point.

"Am I right?" she asked.

The collective of youth group girls nodded their heads, but

I thought I heard Tessa huff beside me. Yeah, my Christian dad cheating on my mom would make me a little cynical too. I hoped Zoe was going to be sensitive to that. But she was right, I had to admit. Even the girls who went to the Christian school weren't immune. Just pulling up YouTube on my phone sometimes exposed me to stuff I wish I could erase from my brain.

"You don't have to have a boyfriend to experience true, deep love," Zoe said. "You can love your friends, your family, your pets even. Jesus said that 'greater love has no one than this, that someone lay down his life for his friends.'"

I wondered if I would ever have friends who would be willing to give their lives for me. I glanced down at my hands in my lap. Izzy sat on my right, Tessa on my left. I hoped they loved me, but sometimes I didn't feel all that lovable.

"Think about this," Zoe continued. "Jesus was never married, and yet would we dare to say He didn't live a life full of love? That He wasn't an example we can follow?"

The room was strangely quiet, and I wondered what the other girls were thinking. I thought about Tessa and Alex and how their romantic attraction for each other actually came out of a friendship that came first. Maybe that's the way it should be.

"Don't ever let anyone pressure you to hurry up and get a guy," Zoe said. "Or that you're somehow going to be lacking love if you don't date or even if you never get married. Because guess what? God has a different plan for each of us. For some it might be finding a husband and having a huge family. For others it might be working hard and being a good aunt, or daughter, or friend. Neither one is better than the other. We're all meant to be examples of God's love to the world. Period. And luckily there are so many awesome ways for us to do that."

I found myself listening closely to her words. This wasn't at all what I'd expected to hear, but I found it strangely comforting. It reminded me of the conversation I'd had with my friends in the cafeteria the other week, about Ms. Larkin being happy, and how I wasn't really interested in pursuing guys the way Izzy and Amelia seemed to be. I had to admit that when Kelsey and Jade had hit me with their zingers, I'd struggled to shake them off.

"When we show pure, Christian love to our friends and family, we're an example to the world of what real love is," Zoe continued, leaning forward, like she really wanted us to get her point. "Girls, don't let the world define love for you. God has already done that by sending His Son."

Chapter
26

I THOUGHT ABOUT ZOE'S WORDS long after I got home, and I thought about them as I lay in bed without Stanley, tears streaming down my face. I know love for an animal is in a different category than love for people, but after hearing Zoe, I felt as though God would at least understand my sadness. Maybe I still didn't fully understand His love for me, but I was trying.

Somehow I managed to get through school the rest of the week without running into Jade or Kelsey, and I even got through drama class without any more "incidents." I'd hoped to catch up with Wilson and finish our conversation about backstage work, but whenever I tried to catch his eye, Amelia or Izzy or someone else would start talking to me. Amelia was especially intent on taking me under her wing, and while it annoyed me in some respects, I could admit she knew a lot about theater and was just trying to help a friend.

But every day I came home to an empty apartment.

I didn't want to ask my aunt how Stanley was doing in his new home. It would hurt too much.

On Saturday I took another shift in the bookstore, this time straightening all the shelves and restocking some of the more popular titles. I was glad for the busywork because I could barely keep myself from stressing about next week's Mason King clinic. By the time school started on Monday, I had psyched myself up and gotten more excited about the event than I felt I could admit to my aunt.

I ran into the bathroom for a pit stop before my first class. I'd had two cups of hot tea, one on the walk over, and had to go pretty badly. I did my business and exited the stall, only to come face-to-face with Kelsey touching up her makeup.

She quickly wiped an errant smudge of lipstick from her teeth and threw the tissue in the trash can. "So I talked with my brother," Kelsey said. "He's a cop."

My pulse jumped.

"He said I could press charges."

I knew exactly what she was talking about, but I decided to play dumb so I wouldn't give her an advantage.

"For what?"

"I had a bruise from where you hit me."

I can't exactly deny I touched her, but a bruise?

"How's it feel never knowing when the cops are gonna come knocking on your door?" Kelsey popped her lips and checked herself in the mirror again.

The bathroom door burst open, and three other girls ran into the stalls, probably hoping, like me, not to be late to their classes. I left Kelsey standing at the mirror, but I felt her presence with me all during World History.

—⁄⁄⁄⁄—

Whenever I really missed my dad, I searched for his name online. It surprisingly yielded a lot of hits. From book covers he'd created to an award named in his honor, there was much to find online about his work as a graphic artist. Sometimes I would be smiling after browsing his pages. Other times I would cry.

Tonight, lying in bed, it was something in between. I pulled up my favorite picture of him on my phone, the one where he was holding my dog, Panda, in his lap. I wondered if he'd be proud of me. I didn't feel proud of myself, but good dads had a way of boosting your self-esteem. They could take your fears and anxieties and somehow lessen them. Sometimes my dad would crack a joke, and it was enough to pull me out of any funk I might be in.

"I miss you," I whispered, swiping to a photo I'd saved of Mason King.

I stared at his face and tried to see myself. It wasn't too hard. My friends had been right. The shared genetics were real. *But what would my dad think about me chasing down this man?*

In the photo, Mason was wearing a gray cowboy hat and a plaid, western shirt, and he rested his arm around a horse's neck. He had just enough flash to seem cool, yet not enough that he looked as if he was trying too hard. He seemed like the real deal, and everything I'd watched confirmed it.

A knock came to my bedroom door, which was still open a crack.

"Come in," I said to my aunt.

She was dressed in sweatpants and a T-shirt. I thought she'd already gone to bed, but maybe she'd stayed up answering emails or reading a book she was considering stocking in the store. Sitting on the foot of my bed, my aunt handed me a photograph.

"I thought you might like to have that," she said.

I stared down at the picture of my parents. Both had their arms around each other and were somehow holding a baby, too.

"That's you," my aunt said.

I obviously didn't remember this moment, but I wished I could. I had no memories of my mom, though sometimes in my dreams I thought for the briefest moments I at least could remember her voice. It was probably just me *wishing* I could.

"I never want to learn how to drive," I said, swiping at my eyes. "They're both gone because of stupid car crashes."

An odd look flashed across my aunt's face. Then it disappeared, and she gave me an understanding smile.

"You're going to do just fine," Aunt Laura said. "No need to rush it, but you'll be ready someday."

I decided to share the photos of Mason King. I turned my phone toward her.

"Do I look like him?"

My aunt took the phone and sighed.

"What?"

"You still want to go?"

I straightened the pillow behind my back. "I have to."

"I just don't want you to be disappointed."

We already had this conversation, right? Is my aunt backing down and changing her mind?

"Your grandparents were not happy."

Great. She told them. "What did they say?"

"It doesn't matter."

"Were they angry?"

Aunt Laura fingered my bedspread, the light from the hall hitting her face and keeping half of it in shadows. I felt like I was seeing a different side of her. She seemed tired, and it hit me that she was experiencing a completely different aspect of all this. I hoped I wasn't creating havoc in her life, but I knew I was.

"When did they first contact you about me?" I asked.

Aunt Laura seemed to know I was referring to my grandparents.

"I didn't find out about your accident until a month after,"

Aunt Laura said softly. "Your father and I occasionally talked, and I'd tried to call him about something book related. I don't even remember what. But his voicemail was full." Aunt Laura stared off into space for a second. "And you know your dad. He never let that happen."

That was totally true. My dad wasn't much of a phone guy in general, but he never let voicemails go unanswered for more than a day or two.

"I got worried," Aunt Laura said. "So I contacted your grandparents. They told me what happened."

"Wow," I said.

"It would've been upsetting either way." My aunt rested her hand on mine for a second. "But that's why I didn't reach out to you sooner. I would have, Shay."

I nodded. I wanted to open up to her, but part of me was ashamed. I didn't really know what my aunt thought about my screwups. *Sure, she took me in, but was it out of obligation? Because she didn't want me to end up in the foster system?* She seemed to care, and in my heart I knew she did, but my doubts got the better of me sometimes.

"I feel like a failure," I finally said.

"Why in the world would you think that?"

I made a sound of disbelief. "Just look at my life."

"Shay."

"No, seriously. Everything has been thrown upside down. I hate school, I'm a burden to you, I keep getting into trouble, and now I've messed things up again by even wanting to go to that stupid clinic."

Aunt Laura tilted her head. "Is that how you really feel?"

"It's true."

I could tell my aunt was thinking hard. Her forehead scrunched up a little, and she reached over to pet Matilda, who was sleeping on my bed. The cat stretched into her touch.

"I can refute all of those things, Shay."

A big part of me wanted her to do just that, but I couldn't really say it.

"I'm going to be totally honest with you," Aunt Laura said. "When your grandmother first asked me if you could stay here permanently, I wasn't at all sure I was ready for something like that." She waved her hand to indicate the apartment. "I mean, I'm rather set in my ways, I had a routine, I was happy. Sharing my space with someone else, especially a teenager, wasn't on the top of my list of life goals."

Her words stabbed me in the heart.

"*But.*" My aunt looked me right in the eyes. "You have been a great joy to me. I was actually *stuck* in my ways, and I needed someone to remind me there's a lot more to life than familiar routines and binge-watching Netflix. In case you didn't realize, that someone was you."

I picked up the photo and just stared at it, only I wasn't really looking at either of my parents. I reached to pet Matilda too. "I miss my dad."

"I know, kid."

"I feel like I'm letting him down."

"He would be proud of you."

I wasn't at all sure that was true, but I let her say it.

"And I don't care what you feel or think, you're not a burden." Aunt Laura stood up. "As far as the clinic, you need to go. If you don't, it's something you'll regret for a long time, and I don't want that for you either. Now get some rest."

My aunt left me alone with Matilda and the photograph. It took me a long time to fall asleep.

Chapter
27

TESSA INVITED ME TO YOUTH GROUP AGAIN on Wednesday, but this time I stayed home. Even though I'd gotten a lot out of it before, I still felt like an outsider—even a little hypocritical considering the mistakes I'd made. I knew none of the girls who attended were perfect, but they were at least less imperfect than me.

At lunch on Friday I sat with my friends and tried to keep composed while I really thought about tomorrow's Mason King event.

"So are you ready?" Izzy asked me when I pulled out my peanut butter sandwich. Today I'd added some honey.

"I guess," I said.

Amelia's eyes widened. "Oh my gosh, I forgot! You're meeting your father tomorrow!"

I grimaced at how loud she said it. She seemed to realize her mistake as soon as she spoke. Her hand went to her mouth. "Sorry."

I checked around us, but no one seemed to be paying attention. As usual. We were definitely not considered one of the popular groups. Drama class students never were, and the four of us especially were such a hodgepodge of personalities.

"Pop quiz," Izzy said.

Tessa stabbed at her salad with a grin. "Not another big word no one has ever heard of!"

Izzy grinned right back. "No, silly, I'm done with that. This time it's food."

"What?" I broke my sandwich in half.

"Food." Izzy took a bite of her pizza. "What's your favorite dessert?"

I grinned. "Will you make it for me if I answer?"

Izzy returned the grin. "I am definitely looking for ideas."

"Banana pudding," Amelia said.

Tessa purred in agreement and added, "I love anything with peanut butter and chocolate."

Izzy was tapping on her phone, probably noting things down in a memo. She looked to me.

"Chocolate ice cream," I said.

Amelia grabbed her napkin. "I think we need to have all of these at the same time."

"Count me in," I said.

"I've never made ice cream," Izzy said. "I bake hot things."

"You should try it."

"I might!"

Amelia pointed at me. "Seriously, what are you going to say to him?"

"I don't know." I might not even meet the man, much less talk to him. I knew what I *wanted* to say. I wanted to tell Mason how I'd admired him for a long time and that I wanted to be like him. I wanted to tell him about my adoptive dad dying and see his response. *Would I be able to tell in his expression whether he knew he had a daughter? Would his eyes mist as he thought about the baby girl he never knew?*

"It's like a movie," Amelia said, eyes widening. "You're Anne Hathaway about to find out you're a princess or—"

"Anne Hathaway?" Izzy pulled a pepperoni off her pizza slice and popped it in her mouth. "Anne is five foot eight with dark hair."

Amelia made a face. "Work with me here."

"And Shay's not about to find out she's—"

"Guys, it doesn't matter," I said.

Tessa and I exchanged glances at the way our friends were so passionate about the arts. I had no idea who would play me in a movie, but it wouldn't be Anne Hathaway, that much I knew. Even if she could un-age herself. I pictured one of those completely unknown girls who the casting agent picks because of her sheer talent. And the movie would jump-start her career, and . . . I smiled to myself. *Maybe I had a* little *drama in me sometimes.*

"I'd want an unknown to play me," I added.

Amelia didn't look convinced. "Not someone famous?"

"You have to start somewhere," I said. "I mean, Scarlett Johansson was an unknown before *The Horse Whisperer.*"

My friends stared at me.

"What?"

Izzy was the first to laugh. "I didn't know you knew any movie facts."

"Figures," Amelia said. "It's about a horse!"

"Even if it is a really old movie!" Izzy continued as though Amelia hadn't said a word.

I loosened up a little at their teasing, but then Amelia got serious again. She lowered her voice. "I think you should tell him who you are."

"Maybe, but . . ."

"I mean, don't you think he'd want to know?" Amelia scooted her chair closer to the table. It grated on the floor. "It really is like a movie, Shay. If I were him, I'd—"

"But you're not," I said, not intending to be mean, but that was the main problem with her idea. I did not have a clue what Mason King would think. *And is it really fair to ambush him like that at a tour stop?*

"How do I even know he'd believe me?" I said, also lowering my voice. "There are probably a lot of girls who wish they were his daughter. Maybe he's even had someone pretend before."

Izzy crunched into her pizza crust, chewing with her mouth open. "All you'd have to do is show him a picture of your mother."

And now I had one, thanks to Aunt Laura, though I didn't know what Mason would think if he knew another man raised his child. I guess it depended on what sort of guy he really was.

"He seems nice in his videos," I said, trying to convince myself I had nothing to worry about.

———✁———

I walked home from school with a smile on my face. My friends had helped ease some of the anxiety I'd been feeling, school was done for the week, and tomorrow I had a date with destiny.

My smile disappeared when I walked into the apartment and my aunt met me with crossed arms. I'd yet to see my aunt truly mad at me. I'd annoyed her when I didn't always clean up after myself, but she'd never raised her voice or been short with me.

When I saw her face, I knew something was wrong.

"I got a call today," she said, then paused, as if waiting for me to guess who it had been.

"Um . . . okay."

"From the mother of one of your classmates."

"Which one?" I pictured Tessa's mom and thought she and my aunt might actually get along.

My aunt shook her head. "I'm doing the talking right now, Shay."

"But you just—"

"It doesn't matter who right now." Aunt Laura's jaw clenched "What happened on your shift two Saturdays ago?"

For one second I had no clue what she was talking about, but then it clicked into place like a dead bolt.

"I . . . did my shift," I said.

That isn't a lie.

My aunt stared me down.

"Why are you asking?" I nearly squeaked.

"Shay, I am expecting you to be honest with me."

I knew she deserved that. And I knew telling lies was not okay. No matter how justified I felt, Dad had taught me that if you couldn't tell people the truth, then you weren't someone they could trust. I wanted my aunt to trust me, but I didn't know how to answer. It's not like I'd been the one to steal from the bookstore.

"Some girls from school came in," I said, dropping my backpack on the floor by my feet.

"Who?"

"I only know two. Kelsey and Jade."

"How do you know them?"

"They're just . . . around."

My aunt took a step toward me, her arms still crossed. "Really? You're really going to make me pry this out of you?"

This? What does she know?

I ran through the ramifications of telling her everything. She'd realize I had covered up the theft.

"Come over here," my aunt said, gesturing toward her laptop open on her desk.

I obeyed.

She woke the computer with a jiggle of the mouse, and I saw what looked like security camera footage on pause. Without a word, my aunt pushed play, and I saw myself appear on the screen with Jade, Kelsey, and the two other girls. There was no audio, but I didn't need it. I knew exactly what happened, and when I saw myself shove Kelsey and her nearly fall over, I felt sick to my stomach.

"Mind telling me what that was about?"

I started to respond, but my aunt kept going.

"Because I am not liking what I'm seeing here." Aunt Laura's voice got a little louder. "And I am very disappointed I'm finding out about this now and that it wasn't from you."

"She was stealing a book. And a key fob."

My aunt dropped down into her chair. "Are you kidding me?"

"I was trying to stop her."

"By shoving her?"

"She . . . touched me first."

Aunt Laura ran her fingers through her hair. Her dyed red streak had mostly faded. "Why didn't you tell me? I could've called the police."

"I paid for them myself."

"What?"

"I didn't want you to lose the money."

"So you were just going to let these girls—" my aunt jabbed her finger toward the computer screen—"get away with this?"

Tears pushed into my eyes. "They threatened to tell the whole school."

Aunt Laura softened slightly at my show of emotion, but I could still see the questions in her eyes. She didn't entirely believe me, and I guess I didn't blame her.

"Tell them what?"

"Everything," I said.

My aunt played the clip one more time, but I couldn't watch. I fell into the sofa, frantically trying to wipe away my tears. I hated to cry in front of people.

"You should have told me," Aunt Laura said.

I nodded.

"But I don't care what they did!" My aunt slammed her laptop closed. "You of all people should know better. What am I going to say if this girl's mother goes to the police?"

"Can . . . she?"

"What were you *thinking*?"

That I am tired of being bullied? That I don't care anymore? That the angry fire rages inside me, and I can't control myself? None of those, save the first, will hold any water with my aunt.

"I'm sorry," I whispered.

"I hope so."

"Do you have any idea how much this could hurt you if they press charges?" Aunt Laura's voice cracked, and I was shocked to see that her eyes looked wet too.

I wanted to throw up.

"I didn't mean to," I said. Matilda jumped on the sofa and tried to get my attention by rubbing up against my arm, but I couldn't move to pet her. Stanley would've come and rested his head in my lap. Thinking about him was almost enough to breach the dam of my despair.

My aunt was right. This could cost me so much more than I ever realized. Why didn't I just let the girls walk out of the store and face whatever they decide to throw my way? It was easy to ask myself now, but I still didn't know for sure whether I'd have any friends left if the whole world knew my history.

"I believe you," Aunt Laura said. "But we're going to have to deal with this."

I walked like a zombie back to my room and leaned against the door, shutting it as I slid to the floor.

Chapter
28

THE POUNDING WOKE ME UP with a jolt. Matilda went flying off
the bed. I sat straight up.

"Shay, wake up, and unlock your door!"

It was my aunt. I could barely see straight, and it was still dark
outside. I climbed out of bed and realized I'd fallen asleep in my
clothes. My hair probably looked like a bird's nest.

I shuffled over to my door and opened it. My aunt was raising
her hand to knock again. She took in my wrinkled clothes and
then glanced at her watch.

"You need to hurry up. You're going to be late."

Matilda moseyed from the room and curled herself around
my aunt's legs. Aunt Laura held a coffee cup and was still in her
bathrobe, but she looked better than I felt.

"Late to what?"

"The clinic!"

"But I thought . . ."

"I said you could go, and I meant that."

"Really?"

"Oh, and your friends are waiting for you."

"Wait . . . what?"

"Shay!"

I peeked down the short hallway and nearly did a double take when I spotted Amelia waving at me. Izzy and Tessa sat on the sofa but stood up when they saw me. I slowly walked over, still half asleep.

"Did you forget?" Izzy asked. She was dressed in horse-themed leggings, her tall boots, and that TARDIS hoodie she loved.

I stared at my friends, rubbing my eyes. I probably looked more like an opossum than a deer . . . caught in the headlights of a FedEx semi.

"Guys, what are you doing here?"

Amelia planted her hands on her hips. "Did you think we'd let you go alone?"

I swung toward my aunt, who'd shuffled into the kitchen to refill her coffee cup. She shrugged. "Don't look at me. It was their idea."

"I'm really still allowed to go?" I wanted to add, *even after last night*?

"Text me when you're there and when you leave."

"Claire's waiting outside," Izzy added.

I couldn't tell if my aunt was happy about this arrangement or not, but I decided I better not look this gift horse in the mouth. But I'd pictured going alone. That way I could really concentrate on Mason and what, if anything, I was going to say. If my friends came along, I doubted I'd get one moment of quiet.

"We've got bagels in the truck," Izzy said. "And I made brownies and chocolate chip cookies!"

"And we'll even make your tea if you hurry up and get dressed!" This came from Tessa, who actually knew where we kept it in the apartment and how much milk I liked in my cup.

I still felt torn by their presence, but it wasn't like they were offering me much of a choice, were they? I'd given up on the idea of attending last night when I cried my eyes out and landed in bed fully clothed. I'd even turned off my phone, so if my friends had texted me about this plan, I never got it.

Ten minutes later I'd changed into clean clothes: my nicest Wranglers, a plaid shirt, and my favorite Ariat boots I'd cleaned and buffed with mink oil and waterproofing salve two days ago.

"About time!" Amelia exclaimed as we said goodbye to my aunt and headed out the back door and down the steps. Tessa handed me my tea in a travel mug, and I smiled to myself. Last night had truly sucked, but with my friends by my side, I felt a renewed excitement over the whole idea of "meeting" Mason King. So maybe I wouldn't have picked this scenario exactly, but it's possible it's actually what I needed.

At least I tried to tell this to myself as we crammed into Claire's truck. Izzy, Tessa, and Amelia were content sitting in the back, so I got the passenger seat beside Claire. Before we even left the parking lot, Izzy was handing out goodies.

"Cookie or bagel?"

"Uh . . ."

"It's not a major decision, Shay!"

"Bagel?"

"What kind?"

I twisted in my seat. A grinning Izzy held up three bags from the local deli. "I didn't know what you guys would want."

My mouth watered. "Plain or egg."

"Oh, my stars," Izzy said.

"What?"

"How did I know you'd pick the most boring flavor?"

I knew she was kidding, but for a moment I felt like she'd said I was boring.

"Hey, you're the one who bought those 'boring' flavors," Tessa shot back with a laugh.

She asked for the cinnamon raisin, and Amelia and Claire had a blueberry. All of them wanted the strawberry cream cheese spread, but I went for the tried and true original. Izzy seemed to know I'd pick that because she had peeled the lid back and stuck a plastic knife in the tub before I could ask.

"Here you go, ladies," she said, handing our prepared bagels up to Claire and me.

"I'm so excited," Amelia said after a minute of bagel munching.

"And he's not even your father," Izzy added.

Whoa. Rewind a little, friends. This was already weird for me, so having them remind me the entire time of Mason's relationship to me wasn't making things easy.

"I'm trying to just go for the clinic," I said.

Claire gave me a quick glance before returning her gaze to the road. I wasn't sure how much she knew about my situation, but I'm sure Izzy had told her something. She was a confident driver, but I was glad she was not allowing herself to be too distracted. Even as she ate her bagel, she kept both hands on the wheel in between bites.

"Sure," Izzy said, mouth full of bagel. "But you can't help thinking about it."

Yep. Even if I wanted to pretend Mason was just another horse trainer, I knew the truth. I knew who he was. *How in the world can I think of anything else?*

I let out an exasperated groan. "I'm so stressed." I slipped down in my seat and filled my mouth with the chewy bagel. Izzy knew the way to my heart, that was for sure.

"So," Tessa said. "I've never been to anything like this. What's it going to be like?"

I told them I hadn't actually attended one either, but I'd been to several rodeos, and I'd seen countless videos online of Mason

King clinics as well as the clinics of other horse trainers. Some were small and intimate. Others were more like what I expected with Mason—a production. They brought semitrucks to hold all their equipment.

"People sign up to have him work with their horses," I said.

"For free?" Izzy asked.

"No, there's some sort of cost."

"Speaking of . . ." Amelia said. "We're paying for you."

I twisted around in my seat again. "No, you're not."

Izzy was nodding her head. "Yes, we are, and you're going to let us."

"But—"

All three of them said my name at the same time.

"You really don't have to," I said softly.

"We want to," Izzy said.

Wow. It wasn't as if the admission price was steep, but I'd had to scrounge for every dollar because I didn't want to ask my aunt after Kelsey and Jade's escapade had cleaned me out.

"Thanks, guys," I said, finishing off my bagel and trying not to feel guilty for allowing them to treat me. First it was the food, now this. I didn't know why, but it was really hard for me to receive, yet it also felt awesome when someone cared.

I got quiet for the rest of the drive to the fairgrounds and just listened to my friends' banter. Amelia and Izzy played the "Name that Musical" game Izzy and her dad had made up, and even Tessa guessed a few right. They knew better than to ask me to participate.

There were more vehicles than I anticipated, at least half being pickup trucks, but Claire found us a spot close enough that we wouldn't have to hoof it too far in the chilly November air. It looked like rain was coming too, and I noticed my friends hadn't really dressed for spending any time outside. It was a good thing the event would be held inside the main arena.

"Gee whiz, this is like a rock concert," Izzy said. "Reminds me of when I saw For King & Country perform here."

I turned to my friend. "You've been here before?"

"Beginning of summer. It was awesome."

I hoped this experience would be just as amazing.

Claire parked and handed Tessa the keys to her truck "just in case" and hopped into the car of her friend, who arrived a minute later to pick her up for some robotics club thing. They'd decided to carpool so Claire could save on gas. She'd be back to drive us home when the clinic was over. We waved her off.

As we walked toward the doors, I tried to laugh and joke with my friends, but I could feel tension working through my stomach like a snake.

Tessa gently bumped me with her shoulder. "It's going to be all right."

I smiled.

"Just relax and try to enjoy yourself." She returned my grin. "We're here to support you no matter what."

I glanced around at my friends. *My* friends. *How could that be?* I came here to Riverbend with nothing but a suitcase and a heart full of grief. It had even felt like God had abandoned me. Yet here I was, surrounded by three girls I met in drama class who really seemed to care about me, even though I couldn't act to save my life and had barely spoken more than a few sentences for the first weeks of our friendship.

And today I was going to meet my father.

Chapter
29

THE SECOND I ENTERED THE BUILDING, I was on high alert for any signs of Mason. His picture was everywhere—snazzy promo posters with some of the photos I had saved on my phone, black T-shirts with his logo embroidered on the pocket, Mason King–endorsed horse treats, and even dog coats that looked like horse blankets.

I felt like a spotlight was on me.

Or crosshairs.

I froze, staring at all the . . . stuff.

"What's wrong?" Amelia said. Izzy had already walked beyond us, wide-eyed and hoping to pet some horses, though I was pretty sure they were in a different part of the building. She'd actually been in 4-H as a kid back in Williamsport, where she lived before coming to Riverbend, and had been the most excited when I told her about visiting the barn near her house.

Tessa and Amelia looked around the lobby bustling with people wearing cowboy hats, Carhartt vests, boots, and jeans. There was a roping cow dummy several kids were intently trying to snag with their lassos. Someone walked a border collie on a leash and harness, though it looked more like the dog was walking them by the way he pulled the leash taut. The chatter of voices droned like a lazy swarm of bees, and still I couldn't move.

"Do you think . . . ?"

It's stupid, really. There is no way anyone will notice.

"What if I really look like him and people come up to me?"

Amelia rubbed her hands together. "Then you just thank them and say, 'Yes, I actually am his daughter.'"

She was only half joking. *I think.*

Amelia and Tessa took me by an arm. "Come on. You're going to be fine," Tessa said.

Izzy came bouncing over, holding up a stuffed horse the size of a cat. It wore a little felt hat, also emblazoned with Mason's logo, and a red bandanna. "Isn't he cute? I wish my brother Bash wasn't too old for it."

"Sebastian may be too old, but *you're* apparently not," I said.

Amelia reached for the stuffed animal. "Oh my gosh, I need one too."

I laughed. *Of all the things to buy, why doesn't it surprise me that my friends are drawn to a plush horse?* I had to admit, even though I told myself *I* was way too old for stuffed toys, part of me wouldn't have minded getting one for my bed. Stanley would've loved it. I could picture him running around the apartment with it hanging from his mouth.

"Okay, where to?" Tessa said, getting us back on track.

"We better find our seats," I said, still searching for any sign of Mason.

Izzy and Amelia went to buy their toys, and I waited with Tessa. Once we were together as a group again, I led the way. People were already inside, but we managed to find seating in the front row nearest the round pen set up inside the huge arena.

I sat down and took it all in.

"Did you text your aunt?" Izzy asked.

Oh, man, I'd forgotten. I whipped out my phone and zapped a text letting her know we were safe and waiting for the event to start. Within a minute she texted back.

Thanks. Have fun!

"Snacks?" Izzy pulled a bag of Peanut M&M's from her coat pocket.

"We just ate breakfast!"

Amelia poured herself a handful. "Hey, never turn down M&M's."

The bagel and tea had gone down easily, but now that I was finally here, my stomach gurgled from the anticipation. No matter how much I tried to calm myself, my insides had other ideas. I didn't want my friends to see how nervous I was, but they likely already knew.

The arena was only half full, but the attendance probably still totaled a few hundred people, most of them women, I noticed. I hadn't seen a horse yet.

Finally, right on time, the event started. Rock music with lots of drums blared from the loudspeakers hanging from the ceiling far above us. Then Mason King made his entrance.

He rode a jet-black horse at a gallop across the arena, and then just when it looked like he was going to run the animal all the way to the other side, the horse did a fast, sliding stop that sent a plume of arena dust into the air.

The crowd broke into applause, and I started clapping too. My friends joined in. Izzy mouthed *wow* to me, and it made me feel good that she appreciated the show of skill. That was my father out there. *That was my* father! It hit me with the intensity of those drums in the music. *What if someday I could join him out there and learn all his amazing techniques? What if I could get so good, I'd have my own clinics and help troubled horses like I'd dreamed of doing since I was a kid?*

A part of me wanted to jump to my feet, point at Mason, and yell, "Hey, world! I'm his daughter! We share the same blood!" Thankfully, the urge quickly left me, but my pulse was still pounding in my ears as he did another lap around the arena at full speed.

"Greetings, Riverbend!" he shouted into his headset microphone. "Are you ready to learn how to truly experience a relationship with your horse?"

The crowd responded with a resounding yes!

I focused on Mason's face and tried to decide if the photos on his website were an accurate depiction. He looked a little older, but his features were hard to see from a distance. I also watched his horse. The big gelding was well-muscled with a long, wavy mane that had to take hours to untangle. He was big enough that he could've had some Friesian bloodlines mixed with quarter horse.

Mason spent a few more minutes taking the animal through a reining pattern including spins and more sliding stops. Like I usually did, I watched the horse as much as the trainer. I didn't know why, but the gelding pinned his ears every time Mason asked for a transition into a faster gait.

Hmm . . . interesting. Horses don't lie. They wore their emotions in their bodies, and unlike humans, did not try to suppress them. If a horse was unhappy, he'd let you know. Sometimes the signs were as subtle as a flick of the tail or a slight raise of the head. But they were there for anyone who took the time to pay attention.

I rested my arms on the ledge separating our seats from the arena, focusing on every word Mason King said. He made a lap around the very outside of the arena. As he approached our seats, my whole body tensed, and Izzy and Tessa both elbowed me, which didn't exactly help me feel relaxed.

"Horses are prey animals," Mason explained. "Humans are predators. Our goal is to teach our horses they don't need to fear us, but they do need to respect us. Without your horse's respect, you have no relationship."

Mason slowed his horse to a trot only a few feet from us, and I got a good view of him and his mount. Sweat soaked the horse's chest and flank, glistening under the lights. His ribcage heaved in and out. A walk break seemed like a good idea, and at first, I thought Mason was going to rest the horse.

But right after he passed us, so close I could see a scratch in the leather pommel of his saddle, Mason cued the horse forward with his spurs. There was nothing wrong with correctly using humane spurs. They were a way to communicate subtly with the horse, but I clearly saw the metal attached to the back of Mason's boot jab harshly into the gelding's side. That's when the horse's ears pinned again.

"Notice how he just disrespected me there when I asked him to move forward?" Mason said through his microphone. "We've gotta nip that kind of behavior in the bud if we're going to have a good partnership. He *must* move his feet when I say move his feet."

Mason immediately pushed the horse into a fast lope, taking another lap around the entire arena. When they passed us again, he slowed to a trot for a few strides before cuing the gelding with his spurs. This time the gelding jumped into the lope, but his tail swooshed.

"See? That's much better," Mason said, and he was met with a round of applause.

Izzy leaned toward me. "The horse seems really tired."

I swallowed. "Yeah."

"Respect is the number one ingredient in a good partnership," Mason said. "Without it, you've got nothing."

I tried to listen as he continued to explain his horsemanship philosophies, things I'd heard many times before in his YouTube videos. But there was something about that horse. On his final lap around the arena, Mason let the gelding walk with loose reins. As they came close to our seats, I looked right into the gelding's eyes and saw nothing but exhaustion and a dullness no video could ever capture. Pinning his ears hardly seemed disrespectful considering how hard he'd worked already for his master.

Mason left the arena, and the applause was so loud I almost wanted to cover my ears. We were given a thirty-minute break to check out the merchandise tables and use the bathroom. My friends stood up to go.

"I'll stay with the seats," I said.

"Are you sure?" Tessa asked.

I nodded.

When I was alone, I tried to understand what I was feeling. Mason talked about respect, and that sounded great on the surface. *So why did his presentation bother me?* A well-trained horse needed to listen to the "asks" of its handler or rider. It was important the horse responded to those cues for everyone's safety. But something rubbed me wrong about it all. I'd looked up to this man well before I knew he was my father. *Was this the way he always was with horses?* Even I could see that gelding was uncomfortable and unhappy. *Had I missed something in the videos?*

It took me five minutes to figure out what nagged me, but as my friends took their seats beside me again, I realized what it was. Respect had to go both ways. *Where's Mason's respect for his horse?*

Chapter
30

"HAVING FUN?" Tessa cradled a cup of vanilla-flavored coffee she'd bought in the lobby.

"Mm-hmm," I said.

Izzy and Amelia were animatedly trying to figure out what band played Mason's entry song, leaving Tessa and me to have our own conversation.

"That hardly sounds convincing."

"I'm fine."

Tessa took a slurping sip, and I knew she wasn't buying it.

"It's . . . he seems different from his videos."

Was it just me? Had anyone else in this place noticed a thing? Maybe I was imagining something that wasn't there or putting a crazy amount of pressure on the man to live up to my expectations.

Before we could talk more, a truck and three-horse trailer from one of his sponsors drove into the arena to another pounding rock song. The next segment was supposed to be a trailer-loading demonstration.

Mason entered the arena on foot this time, followed by a woman in a fringe vest leading a petite, dark-gray horse. The crowd's applause spooked the horse, and it jumped away, slamming right into the woman and nearly knocking her off balance. Mason rushed over and took the horse's lead rope.

"Looks like we'll be working on more than trailer loading today," he said with a chuckle that the crowd echoed. "Go ahead and make some noise!"

As I watched him run the horse around in a circle on the line, my insides twisted every time the horse reacted to the crowd. I would never say I was an experienced horsewoman, but even I knew the animal was terrified.

After twenty minutes of the pre-trailer-loading work, Mason finally brought the horse, a mare, over to the fancy trailer. Just like with the gelding, the mare was out of breath and sweating. The crowd no longer freaked her out, but I wondered if it was because she didn't have the energy to spook.

"This horse refuses to load," Mason said. "Took her owner what? Three hours to load her so they could even get here?"

The lady nodded, said something, and Mason proceeded to point to the trailer with his finger and swing the end of his rope toward the mare's hindquarters to encourage her forward. It didn't surprise me when she balked and actually started backing up instead.

"When they refuse, you gotta make the outside of the trailer uncomfortable," Mason said. "Make the wrong thing difficult, the right thing easy."

I'd heard that phrase used in horse training many times before, but somehow the way Mason was using it didn't seem fair. That mare had just been through an entire training session already. *Now they are going to push her to load as well?*

"So, do horses normally just walk on?" Izzy asked.

"If they're trained to and they feel safe," I said.

"Guess she doesn't," Izzy muttered.

We sat through another hour of Mason working with the mare, but she still wouldn't load. I noticed a few people get up and leave. A man with a beard farther down on our row was dipping his chin to his chest, fighting to stay awake.

Mason had stopped talking and kept pushing the mare, but I think the horse had made her decision—and that was a big "Nope." I almost smiled at her resolve. She definitely had spirit.

"Well, folks," Mason said. "At least she knows who's in charge. We're going to have to call this one and break for lunch."

"Finally!" Izzy said, jumping up.

We bought hot dogs and French fries at the concession stand and took them to a corner of the lobby to eat. Izzy passed around her delicious brownies, and soon our stomachs were full. I unscrewed the lid of my bottled water and took a long swig.

"I really think you should tell him," Amelia said. "There's an autograph line at the end, right? That would be perfect."

"No, it wouldn't," I said.

Amelia cocked her head in that same Labradoodle way that had made me bust out laughing in drama class. Today it just annoyed me. *Does she actually expect me to just get in line and lay it on him when I reach the front?* I'd been sitting on the floor but stood up. "You really think this is a simple, easy decision?"

Amelia stared up at me. Tessa and Izzy looked at each other.

"I mean, seriously?" I waved toward the merch booths plastered with Mason King's smiling face. "This isn't a Disney movie. It's not gonna all end up perfect and happy with a group hug and Mason welcoming me into his family." I crumpled up my hotdog container and stuffed it into the plastic bag Izzy had used for the brownies. "It just isn't."

"I wasn't saying it was," Amelia said.

"But you keep pushing me to talk to him."

"Because I think you should!"

"It's *my* decision."

Amelia clambered to her feet and faced me. "We're all completely aware of that, Shay."

"Then stop pushing me."

"We're just trying to help you!"

"Guys." Izzy got in between us, holding each of our arms.

I yanked mine away. "Stop it, Izzy. I need some space."

Stomping over to the nearest trash can, I stuffed the plastic bag inside as much as I was trying to stuff whatever it was I was feeling. All I knew was that if I kept going, I was going to explode on my friends even more than I already had, and tears were already filling my eyes.

I walked past the booths loaded with overpriced horse tack and just kept walking. Mason was proving who he really was at this clinic, and here I was doing the same.

My phone vibrated in my pocket, but I didn't pull it out. It was probably my friends trying to get me to come back. I wanted to. I really did. But they didn't seem to understand how much pressure I felt.

I wandered past all the hype until I made it outside where the horse trailers were parked. Mason King's tour bus sat nearby too, and I wondered if he rested inside. *Is there anything keeping me from knocking on the door? Is that weird?* I glanced around for security but didn't see any.

The wind swirled around me, and the sky was filling with dark clouds. I stared at the bus, wishing I'd worn my jacket. I'd set myself up for this. Aunt Laura had tried to warn me, but I'd insisted I had to know.

Where does that leave me now?

I closed my eyes for a second and tried to think. I'd tried not to get my hopes up, but if I was being honest, I really had. I'd wanted my aunt to be wrong and her memory of Mason to have faded. It had been a long time ago. Maybe she hadn't remembered right. *And people could totally change, right?* Mason might've been a young, cocky guy when he knew my mother. Didn't mean he'd be like that forever.

With a sigh I shoved my hands into my pockets and stared at the bus. Its generator was running, so someone was probably in there.

I just wanted things to be normal. To have a family again. I'd thought Mason might be my ticket to the life I'd lost. Only now it sounded foolish to have allowed myself to dream like that. Today didn't change anything. I was still the weird outcast who might be able to see a horse's feelings but couldn't make sense of her own.

A sound like a whip cracking startled me, and for a second I thought maybe lightning had struck somewhere in the distance. But then a loud bang, like a hoof hitting metal, followed.

I ran toward the noise. If a horse was loose, it might need help.

His voice struck me first. I rounded one of the pickup trucks to see Mason King and the gray mare in front of a smaller trailer than what had been in the arena. Mason's face was flushed red. He jerked back on the mare's lead, causing her rope halter to dig into her face. At the move, her front hooves came up off the ground, and he yanked down on the halter, presumably as a punishment.

The mare's nostrils flared, and she snorted that strange way horses do when they're scared or upset. She wasn't a big horse—her ears reached no higher than Mason's head. He held a short lunge whip in his right hand and pointed at the trailer. The mare snorted again, and he swung the whip at her hindquarters.

She froze.

In a quick succession that made me flinch, Mason struck the mare with the whip three times, and lash met flesh with sickening snaps. The mare pulled backward to escape him again, her eyes wide, nostrils flaring, but Mason followed her, hitting with the whip.

"Get over it," he said through his teeth, calling the mare a crude name. She tried once more to get away, but he chased after her.

That's when I saw the white patch on her nose, and it hit me like a rock to the head. Her dark-gray coloring, her petite size . . . Ava. This was Ava, the horse I'd met at Green Tree Farm. The little mare with the abscess who'd given me such sweet comfort. *Oh my gosh.*

"Stop!" I yelled. "Just stop it! Leave her alone!"

Mason King didn't even turn in my direction. He gave the mare slack in the lead rope and attempted once more to send her toward the trailer opening. When she balked, he whipped.

It was one thing to see him in the arena from a distance, but it was quite another to be up close, where I could smell the sweaty mare and hear the stinging pain each slash of the whip made on her body. *How long has he been working her out here in private where no one can see his abuse? Why would this mare ever trust another human being again, much less load on any trailer?*

"Leave her alone!"

Ava reared up all the way, shaking her head and yanking Mason's arm up with her as he held on to the lead rope.

I flinched at the stream of profanities he yelled at her as she came back down.

Mason stopped and faced me, and I froze. It chilled me the way he so easily said those horrible words. The anger pulsing from him even as he stared at me. I could *feel* it.

I *had* felt it.

I was instantly back in the bookstore with Jade and Kelsey and saw myself shove the girl. *If her friends hadn't caught her . . .*

"What do you think you're doing?" Mason seethed, dropping a few more choice words.

I stared at the man whose bloodline I shared. *We didn't look much alike on the outside, but where it counted, in our hearts, we were the same, weren't we?*

The mare, her sides heaving, sweat dripping down her neck, hung her head in defeat, and Mason actually dared to smile.

Rain tapped on the metal trailers, and tears filled my eyes. *This was my future, wasn't it?* I started with shoving bullies and ended up abusing a poor animal. Aunt Laura had said the core of who we are doesn't usually change. It was true with Mason, and it was true with me.

"Can someone get security out here?" Mason called out.

"How can you do this?" I said.

Mason turned toward me. "Sorry, girlie, if real horse training makes you cry."

Footsteps pounded behind me, and I didn't wait to be dragged off by some overeager security guard. It wouldn't matter what I said. This was the famous Mason King. A *real* horseman.

I didn't know what to do or where to go, but I had to get away.

I backed up like Ava had, slipping around the trucks and trailers. As soon as I was out of sight, I started running.

Chapter
31

I DIDN'T CARE IF I GOT WET. I didn't care about anything in that moment but escaping Mason King's presence. Soon I was soaked and shivering, yet I didn't stop until I reached the truck. It would be locked, but I couldn't bring myself to go back inside and face my friends.

The downpour eased, but my tears didn't.

I don't know how long I stood there before I felt someone's hand on my back.

"Oh my gosh, Shay, where *were* you?"

Tessa.

"We've been looking everywhere! Why didn't you answer your phone?"

I turned around, not even bothering to hide my crying.

She took one look at me, and her questions immediately stopped. I tried to stammer a response and explain, but any words I might've had disappeared with the rain. I just stood there, and before I could try again, Tessa wrapped her arms around me and pulled me into an embrace.

That was enough to do me in. I lost it and sobbed into her shoulder, holding on to my friend for dear life. I couldn't speak or even breathe normally, but Tessa didn't let go.

"Shay, you're shaking."

I finally broke the hug. "I'm . . . sorry."

She didn't seem to hear me and quickly unlocked the truck. "We've got to warm you up."

"I'm . . ."

I was about to say, "I'm fine," but I wasn't. My teeth were chattering, and my shirt stuck to my back.

"Here, get in." Tessa opened the passenger door and gently guided me into the vehicle. She quickly went around to the other side and started the engine and heater, then pulled her gym bag from behind the seat.

"I always carry a change of clothes." She dug in the bag and produced a T-shirt and sweatshirt. "They're clean," she added.

I didn't really care.

"Get out of that flannel," Tessa said. "I'm serious. You're going to get hypothermic, if you aren't already."

I hesitated, even though my whole body shook. "People . . . will see."

Tessa had a plan for that, too. She produced two towels and hung one across the passenger window, using the window to hold it in place. The other she held up herself, blocking off the windshield and my other side.

Somehow I managed to change into the dry clothes, but I was still shaking. Most of it was from the cold, but not entirely the only reason.

"I'll text the girls and tell them you're safe," she said. "They went back into the arena to look for you."

I managed a nod. "I didn't mean . . . to scare you."

Tessa folded up the towels and stuffed them into the bag. She adjusted the heater vents to blow directly on me. I knew I had some explaining to do, but I didn't even know where to start. You didn't just cry on your friend like that for no reason.

"You don't have to talk to me," Tessa said, looking me in the eyes. "But I care about you. We all do. I know it must've been hard to see your father for the first time like that, and I won't even try to pretend to understand completely, but I'm here, okay?"

My first instinct was to shut down. As usual. But seeing how Tessa had just witnessed me completely fall apart . . . she deserved some trust.

"I can only imagine what you must think of me," I said.

"That you've had a really hard day? Shay, I promise I'm not judging you. It's okay."

"Not just today." I was still shaking and wrapped my arms around myself trying to get warm. "I haven't been a good friend to any of you."

"Hey, I mean it. You don't need to be so hard on yourself." Tessa rested her hands on the steering wheel even though we weren't moving. "You're such a great person, and I wish you could see it."

"Actually, I'm not."

"That's not what I see."

I thought about Jade and Kelsey's dirt and how I'd tried so hard to hide that from everyone, especially my new friends. *But what kind of friendship do I have if I can't share my innermost thoughts? My fears? My whole self?*

I started to tell Tessa why I'd left them in the lobby and how I'd come upon Mason King and the mare. Once I got going, I didn't stop. She looked as horrified as I felt when I told how he was beating Ava. And still I kept talking.

"Remember how upset I got in class?"

Tessa was listening carefully. "Yeah . . . and broke a chair."

"I was picturing the car accident and the last time I'd seen my dad. You asked me if I was angry at God, and sometimes I am. But I'm more angry with myself."

"What in the world for?"

"We were going to a rodeo I wanted to see. My dad was busy, and he had a lot of work to do, but I begged him to go. Finally, he gave in."

"Shay, you aren't—"

"I was in the car too." I wiped at my eyes. "I saw it all, and I'm never going to be able to erase that from my mind."

Tessa was quiet for a second. "Wow."

"And that's not all."

It was now or never. I could dive into the sea of vulnerability and risk the rejection and abandonment I feared, or I could run away from my feelings like I usually did. I knew the choice was mine, and the answer came easier than I thought it would. I wanted my friend to hear this from me, not from Kelsey and Jade.

"Haven't you wondered why I started school later than everyone else?"

Tessa glanced down at the gearshift. "A little."

"It's because . . ." I clamped my arms around myself again to try to get warmer. This was never going to be easy. "I . . . I was in juvie."

My friend's expression went blank for a moment. "Wait, what?"

"Juvenile detention," I said, just in case she didn't get it.

Tessa stared at me, looking like she wanted to laugh at the absurdity. But I knew the truth. The image I'd somehow managed to project to my friends was not who I really was. I was dark on the inside, just like Mason King.

"I'm not kidding. I didn't get released until after school started."

Is it all finally making sense to her? Have I just lost any chance to have a real friend? I didn't wait for her to respond since I wasn't sure if I could handle her reaction. I needed to tell her the whole story.

"After the accident, I was living with my grandparents, and for my birthday they gave me horseback riding lessons." I remembered how excited I was to open up that envelope and see the certificate for a lesson package from a nearby stable. "It was so fun . . . until some of the other girls started making fun of me. I was still so raw emotionally from the accident, and my cuts had barely even healed. One of them called my dad a deadbeat loser, and I lost it."

"Oh, Shay, I'm sorry."

"I punched her."

I couldn't look at my friend as I said the words. I'd immediately regretted it the second my fist hit the girl, but by then it was too late.

I stared at my hands. Hands that had actually hurt someone else.

"She fell down. Hit her head. Concussion."

Amazingly, Tessa just nodded. "But why did you end up—?"

"Her parents are rich, and they wanted me to learn my lesson. They told my grandparents they would sue if I didn't plead guilty. I don't know if they had pull with the judge or not, but I got thirty days."

"That's crazy!"

I shrugged. "Is it? I actually sent someone to the hospital, Tessa. And when I got out, my grandparents had already decided I couldn't stay with them anymore. That's why my aunt took me in. They would've made me move out sooner, but Aunt Laura had to get her apartment ready."

Silence spread through the truck like a fog, and I waited for my words to settle.

"Mason . . . when he was hurting that horse . . ." I'd thought I was done crying, but my tears came again, and I didn't bother to fight them. I faced Tessa. "I'm just like him!"

Tessa pulled her leg up under herself and reached for my hand. "Shay, look at me."

I barely could, but I tried.

"That man we saw in there is nothing like you."

"I put a girl in the *hospital*." I hit my chest with my fist. "Me. I did that."

"You made a mistake," Tessa said.

"And where is it going to stop?" My voice was taking on a frantic tone. "I can't control it sometimes, Tessa. I just get so angry and don't know how to stop it."

Tessa's grip on my hand firmed. "Shay, you're one of the kindest, gentlest people I know. That's your heart."

I started to protest, but she stopped me.

"Are you worthy of forgiveness?" Tessa asked.

"What?"

"Are you?"

"I . . . I don't know."

Tessa smiled. "What I'm trying to say is that none of us is *worthy* of forgiveness. But God is ready to forgive us anyway. We all mess up. I had to learn that the hard way too. Remember . . . real, not perfect?"

"But . . . sometimes it's like a fire inside of me that I can't put out. I don't know what to do."

"You can learn." Tessa squeezed my fingers. "But you don't have to do it alone. A lot of people love you, Shay. Including Izzy and Amelia—and me. We're not going anywhere."

I didn't know what to say. I sniffed and tried to smile. "It's just . . . the way Mason hit that horse . . . so, so angry. These sort of things run in families, don't they? I've got his blood in my veins. How can I fight that? What if it's my destiny to be abusive?"

Tessa shook her head. "We get to choose who we're going to be, and you are *not* your father."

But I'd chosen to hit that girl.

To push Kelsey.

My thoughts started to spiral again, but Tessa wasn't done.

"Family isn't always about blood," she said. "Think about it. You were adopted. It's about the people who raised us and love us for who we really are. Mistakes and all."

A stray tear dripped down my cheek. I wanted to believe her. More than she could know.

"I never had a sister," I whispered, "but if I did, I'd want her to be like you."

Tessa grinned. "Well, you're stuck with me now."

I sat for a moment in silence letting the heater warm me as much as my friend's words. *She really means it, doesn't she?* That she loves me and isn't going anywhere. This isn't a One Act for her or a role she's playing. I could see it in her eyes.

After a minute I told her about Kelsey and Jade finding out and threatening to tell the whole school. Tessa's expression turned firm. "Let them."

"But—"

"The people who matter won't care."

Before we could talk more, the doors to the truck flew open, and Izzy and Amelia both climbed in, flinging a million questions at both of us. After a second, I gathered myself.

"Guys, I'm so sorry for how I acted in there."

They both waved me off, and just like that we were back to being friends. Somehow I'd have to tell them everything I'd shared with Tessa. But for now I just told them what I'd seen Mason King do, and they shared in my horror. Izzy was ready to call the police, but unfortunately, that's not how these things worked. If Ava didn't have any visible marks of abuse, they wouldn't be able to do a thing, and it would be a teen girl's word against a famous horse trainer with a fanatical following.

"Why are you wearing Tessa's sweatshirt?"

I gave my friend a sheepish look. "Uh . . . got caught in the rain."

My phone vibrated in my back pocket, and I decided to check it to avoid another volley of questions.

"Hold on," I said.

There were twelve new texts and three missed calls.

"How many times did you guys text me?"

The missed calls were from Aunt Laura. *That's weird. She rarely calls me.*

Ten of the texts were from my friends, but the other two were from my aunt. I clicked on her conversation thread.

The first came in an hour ago and simply read:

Please call me.

The second text was what had just caused my phone to vibrate. When I read it, I almost threw up.

It's Stanley. He's been hit by a car. Please call.

Chapter

32

I RUSHED INTO THE EMERGENCY VET CLINIC and met Aunt Laura in the lobby.

"Where is he? Is he okay?"

My aunt grabbed me by the shoulders. "Shay."

"No. Please, no."

"It's bad."

"Is he alive?"

"Barely."

My friends and Claire, who'd raced back to the arena for us when Izzy texted her in a panic, entered more slowly and stood off to the side. Izzy swiped at her eyes with a tissue, and Amelia's usual flare for the dramatic was as dampened as my rain-soaked shirt. Tessa whispered to both of them. I couldn't hear what she said.

My aunt sat me down in one of the molded plastic lobby chairs. Maybe I looked like I was going to faint. I felt like it.

"What . . . happened?"

"He jumped the fence while they went out to lunch."

"They left him outside? He hasn't gotten used to them yet. And he's a greyhound! He can't be out in the cold."

Aunt Laura grimaced. "None of that matters now."

I stood up, picturing Stanley's sweet face and how he'd cuddled my leg when I sat on the sofa or burrowed under my covers at night. *Had he been shivering and cold, wondering where I was and why I'd abandoned him with strangers? Was he trying to get back to us and that's why he escaped, or had he simply seen a rabbit or squirrel?* I pictured him darting across the street oblivious to danger, giving the car no time to stop. They might've slammed on their brakes, but there hadn't been time. Stanley hadn't had a chance to escape any more than my dad. "Shay." Aunt Laura was standing right in front of me.

I saw the woman behind the desk in scrubs watching us and tried to shake myself back into the present. Stanley needed me.

"How bad is it?" I sank into the chair again.

Aunt Laura didn't answer me right away, which just confirmed the severity. I didn't know if I could bear it after facing Mason King. *How much more am I going to have to take?* I wanted to cry and scream and curl up into a ball all at the same time. The devastation with my bio father was one thing. I'd chosen to place myself in that position. But Stanley was innocent. He shouldn't have to suffer.

"He's pretty banged up." My aunt let out a long breath. "His back leg . . . I don't think they'll be able to save it."

Oh my gosh. Poor, sweet Stanley. We'd let him down. I knew the organization my aunt volunteered with tried their best to screen their adopters, but they couldn't know everything, and they needed to get the dogs into new homes as soon as they could so they could save more.

"Where is his family now?"

"I've been trying to reach them," Aunt Laura said. "Luckily his chip was still registered with us."

Aunt Laura rubbed a circle on my back, and I appreciated her touch. Her cell phone rang, and she stood to take the call when she saw it was Stanley's owners. My friends rallied around me when she stepped away.

"Guys, let's pray," Izzy said, and Amelia nodded with her.

"I . . . can't," I said.

Tessa knelt down in front of me. "That's why we're here."

"Father," Izzy began, then paused. She took a few deep breaths before she could continue. "We know You care about Shay so much, and Stanley means a lot to her, so I know You care about him, too. He's in trouble, Lord."

I tried not to sob, but my tears wouldn't stop.

"We ask You to help him," Izzy continued. "Show the vet what to do and help him not be in too much pain. Comfort him, and comfort Shay. In Jesus' name."

Everyone said amen, and I attempted to pull myself together. Again. My aunt's voice was getting louder behind us.

"I understand it's a lot of money, but—"

I turned around. My aunt rubbed her temple. *A headache or frustration?* She glanced at me, then quickly looked away.

"Yes, I talked to the vet," Aunt Laura said.

A few seconds passed.

"He's *your* dog!"

My friends and I glanced at one another. It didn't sound like the conversation was going well. *What could those people possibly be saying other than, "We're on our way?"*

Finally, my aunt hung up and looked like she wanted to throw her phone across the room. I went over to her.

"Give me a minute, Shay."

Okay . . .

She stepped outside, and all of us watched her through the

windows. I couldn't read her expression. The wind mussed her hair and flung it into her face, but she didn't move to fix it. She just stared out across the parking lot blinking fast. She had to be getting cold, but still my aunt stood.

I was about to go out and make sure she was okay when she suddenly spun on her heels and came back inside, a resolve in her eyes.

"When are they coming?" I asked.

"They aren't," Aunt Laura said.

I stared at her. "Why *not*?"

My aunt sighed, finally pushing her hair out of her face with both hands. She yanked a hair elastic from her pocket and tied it into a ponytail.

"They want him put down," she said.

Izzy gasped and reached out and touched my arm in reassurance, but I was not ready to be reassured. I wasn't ready for anything close.

"They . . . can't do that!"

"His surgery and everything would cost close to two thousand," Aunt Laura said. "They don't have the money."

"That's a lie! You saw their house. They have enough for that!"

"Shay."

"I can't, Aunt Laura. Please. We have to help him."

Aunt Laura took in a long breath and let it out slowly. "I need to talk to the vets again, but I promise I'll do everything I can."

"They can't abandon him like that," I whispered.

One of the vet techs came out and looked expectantly at Aunt Laura. She waved me over. "Can my niece see him?"

The tech hesitated, checking over her shoulder, and then gave us a nod.

I left my friends in the lobby and walked down the long corridor past exam rooms. *How could a place that healed also be a place where animals died?* Antiseptic met my nose, and I tried to breathe through my mouth. It wouldn't help Stanley if I puked.

"We have him on pain meds," the vet tech said.

I tried to prepare myself for what I'd see, but when she opened the stainless-steel cage on the bottom row of a dozen similar cages, I felt nauseated. Stanley lay on his side, his fur matted with dried blood. It looked as though they'd tried to clean his scrapes, and black stitches poked from a wound on his shoulder.

Dropping to my knees, I climbed halfway into the cage before anyone could stop me. Stanley didn't even lift his head.

"Careful, Shay."

I gingerly touched his ear, and his tail quivered and then gave a little thump.

"Oh, boy . . ." I let my tears fall as I stroked him. "It's gonna be okay."

His back leg was covered with bandages, but blood soaked through the gauze. *Isn't there any way to save it?* I knew dogs could get by with three legs, but I just felt so sad that this greyhound, born to run, wouldn't be able to. At least not the same way. It wasn't fair.

I wanted to hold him and make sure he knew I wasn't ever going to abandon him again, but I didn't want to hurt him any more than he already was. After a few minutes the vet tech suggested we let him rest, and I reluctantly extracted myself from the cage.

"Stay strong," I said to the dog. "You can do this. You're not alone."

—m—

Aunt Laura was on her phone again with the adoption organization the second we got back into the lobby. I wanted to stay in case anything changed with Stanley, but she reassured me he was stable and asked Claire and the girls to take me home. I felt like she needed the space to figure all of this out alone but couldn't say it. I was also about to fall over with exhaustion.

In the apartment I didn't ask my friends to hang around, but they did on their own.

"We're staying," Izzy said, and the others agreed. Tessa's mom would pick them up later.

I couldn't offer anything but my exhaustion. As I slumped on the sofa and my friends joined me, I was amazed it didn't matter. They'd seen me at my worst today, and they were still here.

Sitting there in my aunt's tiny living room, I told Izzy and Amelia what I'd shared with Tessa in the truck, hoping they'd be as understanding. When I was done, I waited for their responses.

"Thank you for trusting us," Izzy finally said.

"I wish I could go back and change things," I said.

Tessa, who was sitting on the opposite end of the couch from me, leaned forward so she could catch my eye. "We just don't want *you* to change."

"Right," Amelia agreed.

"Because we love you exactly like you are," Izzy said.

That made me chuckle. "Even if I can't act?"

"Well . . ." Amelia started, then grinned at me so I knew she was kidding.

"Even if my father is a jerk horse trainer?"

"Um, yeah," Izzy said adamantly. "Because you aren't him." She slapped her leg. "I think we should do something to put that man in his place."

We spent the next few minutes imagining silly scenarios that would do just that. Like if he had toilet paper hanging out of his pants during a clinic, or if someone "accidentally" put laxative in his coffee. Or a melted chocolate bar on his saddle. Izzy's little brother must've rubbed off on her because she came up with most of them. They were silly, childish things that we knew were totally inappropriate, but in that moment, I needed to laugh, and somehow picturing Mason King sitting on a whoopee cushion made me feel better.

There wasn't much to eat in the apartment, but Izzy found the ingredients for peanut butter cookies. She busied herself baking a tray of them, which we ate with milk while binge-watching one of Izzy's favorite baking shows.

By the time my aunt got home, I felt like I could at least face reality.

She dropped her keys and phone on the kitchen table.

"They're taking Stanley to surgery on Monday," she said.

My friends and I glanced at each other, and then Izzy shot her fist into the air and Amelia whooped.

"Wait, does that mean . . . ?"

"They're giving him back to our organization," Aunt Laura said.

"But the bills, how are—?"

"I don't know yet, but the vet is going to work with us."

My aunt looked about as tired as I felt. The skin under her eyes was dark, and her shoulders slumped. She shuffled over to the coffee maker, but I intercepted her and gave her the biggest hug I'd ever given someone outside of Tessa today.

"Thank you," I whispered.

She hugged me back.

Chapter
33

I WALKED INTO SCHOOL ON MONDAY and instantly realized everyone knew. The surreptitious glances. The whispers. It felt like everyone was staring at Shay Mitchell.

But now that the word was out, it wasn't what I expected. A guy with long hair everyone knew sold weed actually nodded at me. A girl from marching band pointed her phone at me with a thumbs up, and another girl who always came to school on her skateboard made eye contact when she normally ignored me.

It wasn't all positive though. Some crew-cut dude I thought I recognized from Chemistry made an L with his fingers as I walked by, and someone "accidentally" jostled me in passing.

I made it to my locker and did my best to remember what Tessa said about the people who mattered not caring. It's not like I was the only girl here who'd gotten in trouble before, but after this weekend I didn't have the energy to face much more.

I dropped my backpack in my locker and pulled out my World History textbook. Stanley was alive, and that's all I really cared about. I could deal with the rest. Somehow.

"So. How's it feel?"

Turning around, I faced Kelsey and Jade.

"How does what feel?" I asked.

"Being the talk of the school's a big deal, you know." Jade pulled out her phone and took more shots of me for her Instagram. I didn't want to know what the captions would be. A flicker of that familiar anger tried to rise up. Rather than fight it, I took a second and just felt it. *Okay, so I'm angry. It's what I do with the feeling that matters, right?*

It was a struggle to keep my cool, but I was determined. "I don't mind as much as I thought I would," I said.

The girls glanced at each other, and I almost smiled. I think I threw them off.

"Everyone knows what a loser you are now," Kelsey said.

"Of course, we knew that all along," Jade added.

"Hmm. Guess you did. Gold stars for both of you."

Jade pocketed her phone, and Kelsey let out a little laugh that didn't seem as confident as before. "Everyone *knows*, Shay. Everyone knows you were in *juvie*," Kelsey said, saying *juvie* loud enough for the kids around to hear.

"Good. I'm glad."

They both stared at me for a second, as if they were dogs encountering their first porcupine. Maybe they wanted to swoop in for the kill, but one look at my quills and they hesitated. I almost laughed at my silly analogy. I'd have to share it with Izzy later. I crossed my arms, feeling bolder. I held my textbook to my chest. "Now you have nothing on me. Did you think about that?"

Before the girls could respond, Tessa, Izzy, and Amelia were standing beside me.

Izzy reached out her hand. "Hey, there. I'm Izzy. And you must be the girls who thought it was a good idea to bully my friend."

Kelsey looked at Izzy's outstretched hand like it was a lizard.

Tessa rested her arm on my shoulder, and Amelia did the same on the other side.

"If she's a loser, then we all are," Amelia said.

"Got that right," Kelsey muttered.

My friends smiled their sweetest smiles and stood there surrounding me. For the first time in a long time, I felt like maybe things were going to be all right.

"I love being a loser," Izzy said, and for some reason that made her giggle. Then her giggles spread to Amelia and Tessa, and as the three of them laughed like hyenas, I began laughing too.

Kelsey and Jade backed up, as if whatever silliness disease we had was contagious. Maybe it was.

Alex spotted us from down the hallway and ran over. "Hey, did I miss the party?"

Chad and Wilson joined us a few seconds later, along with two other girls from drama class. And before we knew it, all of us were making such a scene laughing over nothing, I worried someone would call the principal.

When I finally caught my breath and looked up, Kelsey and Jade were gone.

—⁂—

I lay in bed that night with my phone. I pulled up YouTube, and the first recommendation was a new Mason King video. The thumbnail showed Mason loping on his black gelding, fringed chaps and cowboy hat making him look like a cowboy from the Old West.

Maybe someday I'd go back and rewatch the videos I used to enjoy. Maybe someday I'd attend another clinic and tell him who

I really was. And maybe someday I could look at his face and not recoil in disgust.

But today I unsubscribed from his channel.

Stanley's surgery was successful, I texted my friends.

The vet had called Aunt Laura at dinnertime to let her know Stanley was waking up and recovering nicely. He was still doped up on pain meds, but it wouldn't be long before they weaned him off those.

> Izzy: I'm so glad!!!
>
> Amelia: I was praying it would be. 🙏🙏
>
> Tessa: Me too.
>
> Me: Thanks, guys.
>
> Izzy: When is he coming home?

Good question.

> Not sure, I responded.
>
> Amelia: I've been thinking about the Christmas play.
>
> Tessa: No! LOL
>
> Izzy: UGH. ☺
>
> Amelia: Wait!!! Hear me out!!!

I didn't want to shut down my friend, but I wasn't in the mood for arguing about drama class. Amelia's exuberance might fit perfectly on her, but I couldn't seem to wear it.

> Amelia: I've decided to do it myself. A one-woman Christmas One Act. I have three to choose from. All proceeds will go to Stanley's vet bills.
>
> Izzy: What???
>
> Tessa: But how?
>
> Amelia: Don't anyone try to stop me! It's already

in the works. Ms. Larkin's helping me, and we're looking for a time on the school calendar.

Izzy: I'll make cupcakes to sell!!!

Tessa: Mom and I can design posters.

I stared at my phone. *Really? They are serious?*

Aunt Laura hadn't gotten into many of the financial details with me, but I knew the adoption organization wouldn't be able to cover all the bills. When I'd tried to ask her about it, my aunt had told me she'd find a way, even if she had to sell half her inventory.

My phone blew up with my friends' ideas. I gave up trying to answer. All I could do was watch their texts fly. After a few minutes I finally got in a response:

Me: Wow. You guys are so sweet!

Izzy: Not as sweet as Stanley.

Later, after I turned off my light and my phone, I stared up at the ceiling. I still didn't know if Kelsey's parents were going to press charges against me, since I'd found out it was her mom who called my aunt. It was possible they wouldn't since my aunt had divulged the info about Kelsey stealing from her store. But if they did, one thing I knew for sure. My friends were going to be there.

Chapter
34

THE NEXT DAY TESSA DROVE ME to Green Tree Farm after school. I'd finally talked to Aunt Laura about maybe working there some mornings, and she agreed to at least let me talk to Janie about it again.

As we walked toward the barn, a few snowflakes drifted from the sky. I stopped, opened my mouth, and tried to catch them.

"You're a goof," Tessa said with a laugh.

Janie met us outside the barn. "You're also late."

"Sorry. Traffic."

This time the horses had been brought in for the night, so as we meandered down the barn aisle, the horses popped their heads over their Dutch doors. A few nickered when they saw Janie, probably hoping it was time for grain.

In the last stall, at the opposite end of the barn, Ava stood in the back corner of her stall, just like when I'd first met her. When I saw her face, a pang of guilt hit me.

"I'm so sorry I couldn't stop him from hurting you," I whispered to her.

The mare saw us and came over. There were no marks on her body from where Mason had whipped her, but sometimes scars ran deeper than that.

Ava nuzzled Tessa's coat.

"She's beautiful," Tessa said.

"Can't believe her idiot owner took her up there," Janie said, never one to mince words. "I would've told her to save her money and let me help."

"Ava was terrified," I said.

"Don't doubt it."

"I'm glad she's here at least."

Janie rested her hands on her ample hips. "Yeah, well, not for long."

My heart sank. "What?"

"For sale." Janie shrugged. "I've half a mind to buy her myself and start that lesson program you got me thinking about."

I took in the mare's face, her kind eyes, and was amazed how she could totally live in the moment. Humans had mistreated her, yet here she was trusting us. Sure, she'd probably have flashbacks next time someone tried to load her, kind of like the moment I'd freaked out in drama class, but for now she was content to be present. Here. Now.

"You should totally do that," I said softly. "I think she's got a lot to teach people."

I waved to Tessa and climbed the back stairs up to the apartment. Seeing Ava had given me a little closure about that terrible experience at the clinic, but it also reopened my Mason wound. I'd probably be thinking about him a lot.

"Shay? That you?"

"Yeah!"

"We're in the living room!"

I dumped my backpack in my room as I passed it. *We?*

My aunt was sitting on the sofa. When she saw me, a huge grin spread across her face. Lying beside her with his head resting in her lap, a blanket over him, was Stanley.

I don't think I've ever run so fast in my life. I was in front of them in practically two strides. Stanley's tail thumped and wouldn't stop. His ears went back, and he shifted, trying to get up and greet me.

"Whoa, whoa," Aunt Laura said. "Settle down there."

I fell to the floor and kissed his head, gently rubbing his ears and trying oh so hard not to cry again. But I couldn't help it.

"I told you it was gonna be okay," I said through my tears, and Stanley licked my face, which made me laugh and cry at the same time.

My aunt lifted the blanket off the greyhound, and I sucked in a breath and started crying even more when I saw the massive cast on his back leg.

The leg she'd said he'd lose.

"But . . . how . . . ?"

"It was touch and go, but they were able to save it."

I covered my mouth with my hand and couldn't say another word.

"Surprised?" Aunt Laura said, wiping her own eyes with her fingertips.

I nodded, wanting to hug her and Stanley both.

"I didn't want to get your hopes up," Aunt Laura said. "That's why I didn't tell you right away. And we weren't sure if we'd have the money, but someone generously donated the funds."

Stanley tapped his tail again, edging closer to me on the sofa. I could still smell the bandaging tape and antiseptic vet smells.

And I didn't care in the least.

I buried my head in his neck. *Thank You, Lord.*

"Really?" I muttered into his fur.

"Shay, the donor wanted to remain anonymous, but I think you should know who it was."

I pulled back and held Stanley's head in both my hands. Whoever it was, I owed them big time.

"Your grandmother."

I glanced up suddenly at my aunt. "What?"

"She wanted to help. She wanted to help you, Shay."

I stared into Stanley's gorgeous brown eyes, quickly overcome with appreciation that Grams cared, but sadness, too, that she hadn't reached out to let me know personally or reached out at all since I'd arrived here. But maybe this was her way, and I decided it was enough for now.

In a few moments Stanley was asleep, and I sat up and planted myself on the sofa too.

"How long does he get to stay here?"

"Well . . ." Aunt Laura re-covered him with the blanket and rested her hand on the greyhound's side, careful to avoid his scrapes.

My aunt's hesitation dampened my joy. "Sorry," I said. "I know he'll go up for adoption once he heals."

"No, Shay." Aunt Laura stroked Stanley's head. "He's never going up for adoption again."

I stared at my aunt. She stared back. Then she grinned at me.

I was not the type of girl to scream or squeal. I never had been. But the sound that came out of me made Stanley open his eyes again.

"Oh my gosh, are you serious?"

"He's staying right here," my aunt said, reaching over and patting my shoulder. "And so are you."

"Did you hear that, Stanley? You get to stay!"

His tail wagged again, and I think he knew. We were both a little beaten up, a little bruised, but somehow, we'd made our way home to our new normal here in Riverbend.

I had to admit, it felt really good.